Astraphobia

The Paranormal Canadiana Collection
Saskatchewan

Print ISBNs
Amazon print 9780228635376
Ingram Spark 9780228635383
Barnes & Noble 9780228635390
BWL Print 9780228635406

The Paranormal Canadiana Collection
Copyright 2025 BWL Publishing Inc.
Copyright 2025 by Paul Grant
Editor S. Peters Davis
Cover artist Michelle Lee

Dedication

To Laurie

The Paranormal Canadiana Collection

2025 Releases

Night at the Legislature – Manitoba – Author Nancy M. Bell

Shúhta Dene – Northwest Territories – author Maureen Gresl

Dancing Mary – British Columbia – author Jay Lang-Young

Astraphobia – Saskatchewan – author Paul Grant

Twice born – New Brunswick – author Graeme Smith

Playtime – Prince Edward Island – author Eden Monroe

2026 Releases

Ghosts of Bell Island - Newfoundland - Eileen Charbonneau and Jude Pittman

Black Gold Eye - Alberta – author JD Shipton

Haunting the Klondike - Yukon – author Joan Donaldson-Yarmey

Cardinal - Nova Scotia – author donalee Moulton

The Deepest Divide - Ontario – JC Kavanagh

Metamorphe - Quebec – author Juliet Waldron with John Wisdomkeeper (posthumously)

Table of Contents

Prologue

Nairn, Scotland 1889

Nairn clung like a barnacle to the rocky, wind-blasted Scottish coast, pounded by thirty-foot seas, nor'easters full of ice and snow all the way from Lapland, and all the other furies and favours conjured by Poseidon. You had to be strong to live there, whether you fished the angry ocean, farmed the scrawny land, or ran businesses that saw to the needs of the fishers and farmers. There weren't ten thousand souls in the whole of Nairnshire because the land was so poor, yet people had been living and working here since the Norse came ashore in 1,000 AD. For three centuries people made the best of their meagre place in the great scheme of things, looked out for one another and managed to get by. The constant wind gave their faces a fresh-scrubbed look and leaning into it every day made them tougher than most.

Ten-year-old Robert McKenzie loved the wind, loved the violence of it, the way it billowed his cheeks, flapped his coat and almost lifted him off the ground. It would be another decade before the Wright Brothers took flight near Kitty Hawk on the windy North Carolina coast of America, so for now, flying was still for the birds alone. But a boy could surely dream with his arms stretched wide like wings, feet on tippy toes as he leaned into the gale while taking care not to get tossed into the sea.

From his front walk, Hamish McKenzie watched his son deep in play on an April afternoon. They were clearly father and son – stocky, sturdy, with tousled, rusty hair over a ruddy, freckled face, a pug nose, and the bluest eyes you've ever seen. Robert still had the innocent shine of youth while Hamish carried the scars of moral battles won and lost, paths not taken, deeds he wished undone, and deals with the devil that had to be made.

He was a good man now, or at least tried to be. But there were some dark days when he first set out to find his way in the world, days he'd just as soon forget. Work was scarce back then, so he traveled the length and breadth of Scotland for more than a year doing odd jobs and day labour until he made his way down to northern England and found work on the Liverpool docks. Britain was the greatest trading nation in the world, and every berth along the River Mersey was full, and the docks and gangways were bustling. As soon as a ship's cargo was unloaded, more cargo was brought on board, and the ship steamed out to sea while another was guided into the dock to take its place. The vessels carried palm oil from West Africa, lamb from New Zealand, timber from British North America, textiles and spices from India and Asia, and who knew how much contraband.

The men who worked the cranes, cranked the winches, and hefted the sacks and crates were rough and ready for anything. Their place of work was tailor-made for smuggling drugs and stolen goods – a packet of opium, a barrel of whisky, sacks of coffee beans, and bales of tobacco were spirited away and sold privately within the day, the loss put down to 'slippage.' After work the men made straight for the pub to drink, eat, play at dice and chase after women. Hamish lost his pay cheque several times before he got wise to the rigged dice games. To pay off his gambling debts he helped men hide cases of rum, wheels of cheese, bolts of silk and satin. Sometimes the cargo was humans, dark-skinned, wide-eyed, and wary as they were led off the boat in chains.

Hamish feared that if he refused to help in these illegal enterprises, the men would beat him or even kill him for the secrets he knew. So, he followed them in their exploits and committed crimes he tried not to remember, some too unspeakable to put a name to. He was awash in shame every time he thought about his actions during those few years, so he buried the knowledge deep enough that it would never again become exposed.

Now he was a respected butcher, the owner of McKenzie's Meats on Thurlow Road, a man with money in the bank, a good house, a wife, and a strapping young son. He was a deacon in the Presbyterian church, a man who gave money and meat to feed the poor. Much as he'd like to play in the wind or kick a football with his son, his pursuits were now sober and serious, as befit a man of thirty-seven years. But on a windy spring afternoon, he could be a boy by proxy as he watched his firstborn try to fly. Stout as he was, even Hamish found it hard to keep his footing in the stiff breeze. Offshore, a towering black storm was coming in fast, lit from within by shimmers of lightning.

"Come in now, laddie," Hamish shouted to his son. "*Na buaireadh na diathan*," as we used tae say. "Don't tempt the Gods." Hamish had a good set of pipes, and he hollered loud enough to be heard in Kingsteps, but the wind tossed his words away like bits of paper. And anyway, Robert wasn't listening, flying as he was in his own mind at least, the wind flattening his hair and roughing his ruddy cheeks. And then everything stopped – the wind, the sea, the sky itself – and the world held its breath for a moment too long.

"Come now, Rabbie," Hamish called into the calm. "Let's get out of this weather and have a cuppa tea." Robert heard his father call his name and turned just as the lightning bolt struck and Hamish McKenzie ceased to exist. He stood rigid for half a moment, welded to the spot as his electrical system was short-circuited by fifty million volts coursing through his body. He was dead before he collapsed on the ground like felled steer.

Robert ran crying to his stricken father and threw himself on the smoldering body, oblivious to the crackle of electricity around him or the danger of another strike. Maura McKenzie had been watching from the window and now ran weeping out of the house to snatch Robert away from her dead husband, out of the wind and away from the lightning. There was nothing she could do for poor Hamish now. Her only sensibility was to shelter Robert from the storm.

Maura McKenzie was not a flibbertigibbet, nor was she given to idle chit-chat, gossip, superstition, or fear. She was canny and not easily gulled. As a nurse, she'd seen the bloody side of life, and as a result, she was good in a pinch, calm and rational while others fussed about to no avail. But pragmatic as she was, she knew the old beliefs were not to be ignored. Myths were merely truths learned through the ages and disguised as allegory. Wasn't Hamish the firstborn and isn't it true that the firstborn are chosen for death by lightning? Millions of people in India believed that to be true. Native North Americans tremble before the wrath of Thunderbird, and the Incans of South America fear Illapa, the god of war and weather, including lightning. Call them by whatever name you like – Zeus, Vulcan, Thor, Astrape, Perkwunos – but when they hurl the bolt at you, it is with the finality of all time. She thought of the *Bible*, when the Lord appears in *Zacharia*: "Then the Lord will appear over them; his arrow will flash like lightning." Maura knew her *Bible*, knew of the many ways the Lord sends down His Judgement on the wicked. The Gaels say that *Dealanach* is never wrong, that lightning doesn't lie. Could it be true for Robert too? Could the lightning return to this place and strike down her firstborn son as well? So after Hamish was buried, Maura wrote to George Clendenning, an old family friend now living in Canada:

My dear George: You have not perhaps heard yet of the death of my husband, Hamish McKenzie, this past month. He was struck dead by lightning and so has left me a widow with a wee bairn to raise and an abiding fear that perhaps Robert may also fall prey to the McKenzie Curse of death by lightning. My aim is to emigrate to Canada. Could you suggest a place in that great country

George Clendenning and his wife, Margaret, lived in a rambling house on a well-watered acreage near Stanley Corners, southwest of Ottawa. The place was purpose-built for a big family with kids and dogs running around the place, savoury aromas coming from the kitchen, and plants and science projects constantly cluttering up the tabletops and windowsills.

But Margaret died giving birth to their daughter, Rona. Bereft, George lost himself in his business affairs and let a series of nurses and governesses see to Rona. As she grew, Rona and her father rubbed along like two roommates leading parallel lives. So, when Maura's letter arrived, George began to hope that, if they shared the house with another partial family, everyone might be better off, especially Rona, who would have a woman to learn from and confide in. With that in mind, he quickly wrote his response:

Maura sold McKenzie Meats at a fair price to Hamish's two assistants, auctioned off the house and furniture and bought passage for herself and Robert aboard The Lady Anne, a ship in the White Star line. Fifteen days later they sailed up the St. Lawrence and disembarked in Montreal. A train took them to Ottawa the next morning, where George and Rona met them. On March 21 – the first day of the spring of 1890 – Maura and Robert McKenzie began their new life in Canada.

*Winter   thunder   bodes
summer hunger.*
-Proverbs of Scotland (1868)

– Alexander Hislop

Chapter 1

The photograph on the front page of the February 1915 edition of *The Prairie Farm and Home* newspaper showed a handsome stud called The Off-Side Wheeler, standing 17.3 hands high and weighing "...considerably more than two thousand pounds...". GIANT BELGIAN DRAFT HORSES SET A NEW MARK, the caption proclaimed, and the article beneath praised the beautiful and gentle Belgians, which were raised by Walter H. Hanley of Providence, Rhode Island.

The horses intrigued Robert McKenzie, and he considered buying a pair to breed at Home Farm. He'd done well since moving his young family to Saskatchewan a decade earlier. He was a successful grain farmer and rancher who could spot good breeding stock better than most, and he was interested in acquiring a breeding pair of draft horses. He very nearly bought a pair of Percherons from the fire department a few years back when they started using motorized fire trucks. The Percherons were lovely beasts, dappled white and gray and standing more than 16 hands. They were calm and tractable and would have been useful on the farm, but some small voice in his head advised him against it. A few dairymen in the city bought the fire horses to pull their delivery wagons, and as expected, they were ideally suited to the job – patient, steady, and good with children, who always wanted to pet them. But the first time the fire bell went off, the horses galloped off to the fire hall ready for duty, leaving a trail of broken bottles and spilled milk in their wake. It was impossible to predict when the fire bell would ring, so the dairymen reluctantly took the horses out of service.

These Belgians, though, looked to be fine animals – strong and even-tempered. The question in Robert's mind was, how would they adapt to the Saskatchewan climate, which was so much colder than pleasant Rhode Island? He sat down to write a letter to Hanley inquiring about the cost and availability of breeding stock, but his attention was distracted by a rhythmic squeak and a sing-song voice growing louder outside. He looked out his office window on the second floor of his home to see a small dark man walking up the drive beside a wagon pulled by a feather-footed chestnut horse deep across the shoulder and wide across the back. Not as handsome as The Offside Wheeler, but a fine-looking animal just the same.

Robert went out onto the front verandah and watched as the little procession wandered into his farmyard. Rumbling clouds scudded in from the northwest, rattling the bare branches of the trees and stirring up dust devils in the farmyard as the man continued his ditty.

"Spare the rod and share the blame. Watch the world go up in flames. Your protection or your shame. Take the rod and fire's tamed."

He repeated the verse a few more times to the beat of the squeaking cartwheels until the little procession came to a halt in front of the house. On the side of the cart was a hand-lettered sign:

A. Thorson Lightning Rods

"No rod, I see," said the man without any preamble. He looked McKenzie up and down, then turned his gaze to the rooftop. "No rod at all. Not so good for a building so tall."

"How can I help you, sir?" Robert asked. There was still a Scottish burr in his speech, as well as a touch of impatience. He wanted to get back to the Belgians and his correspondence with Hanley, not be distracted by a travelling drummer, especially with a storm approaching.

"Help *you*, more like," said the man, looking at the darkening sky. "Name is Thorson. Son of Thor. I can offer you much more. Protection from the fiery sky. That's the truth, sir, not a lie."

"Protection? From the sun? Are you peddling parasols?"

"Lightning, dear man. So frightening, unplanned. In that, Arne Thorson is humbly your man." He gave a low bow.

"How in the name of all that's holy do you protect me from lightning? It goes where it wants to go."

"These rods provide a cone of protection. Send the flash in a different direction."

"Stop talking in riddles, man, and state your business."

"The copper rod is placed at the peak, the highest point of your roof. There's a storm coming soon that will give you the proof. You see a rod's fixed to my little cart's roof," he said, gesturing grandly to his glorified Red River cart with a small copper lightning rod bolted to the top. The American inventor Benjamin Franklin made part of his fortune peddling lightning rods, but McKenzie was not convinced by this salesman. His own father was killed by lightning. He'd seen it with his own wide eyes. Why should he seek out lightning and attract it to his home?

"You're telling me that if I stick that stick on my rooftop, it will attract lightning?"

"Yes, sir I do. Would you like to buy two?"

"I would not like to buy any, sir. Why would I want something that will ensure that my house is struck by lightning? Begone, sir." The image of his father dead on the blasted ground was seared onto his eyelids for all time. Robert loved the wide-open prairies, but he cursed the summer lightning that terrified the livestock and sometimes set crops afire. He wanted nothing to do with lightning or this little man, but Thorson moved closer to the verandah and smiled to reveal gleaming white teeth incongruous in such a weathered face.

"The rod will save you. Yes, you'll see. I'll even give it to you free. Just pay my installation fee." He didn't quite dance a jig but hobbled from foot to foot as if he stood on hot coals.

"Not a chance. Off with you now." McKenzie turned to go back inside.

"If you refuse to see it," Thorson scowled and narrowed his green eyes, "then on your own head be it. *In tuo capite fiat.*"

"Is that some kind of curse, sir? How dare you..." Robert said as he started down the front stairs to give the man a thrashing and send him on his way. But Thorson had already turned his horse and cart around and was halfway down the driveway, singing his little song again to the beat of the squeaking cartwheels.

"Spare the rod and share the blame. Watch the world go up in flames. Your protection or your shame. Take the rod and fire's tamed. Spare the rod and share..."

As he watched Thorson vanish into the gathering storm, Robert pulled out his pipe, struck a wooden match on his thumbnail, and shook the silly rhyme from his brain. He had planned a trip into town that evening to attend a benefit for an outgoing police officer. Chief Walter Johnson himself was presiding over the festivities, so the night promised to include plenty of booze and girls. Janet had all but lost interest in that side of life, and Robert still had a bit of the tomcat in him so he considered it no more than his due to let loose every now and again. Truth be told, Janet was relieved. But it would be a bad night to be out in an open car. Roiling clouds muscled their way across the landscape and a chill wind promised rain from the Dakotas to the southeast. Robert thought that there was almost nothing good about a wind. It stole topsoil, tipped over bins, and flattened barns. He loved it as a child and delighted in its capricious violence, but now he felt impotent against its power to destroy what he had built, so he cursed and feared it.

Robert thought back a decade to the series of events that had brought the McKenzie family out west to begin with, starting in 1905 with the creation of a new province – Saskatchewan...

Chapter 2

Wednesday, September 6, 1905

Province of Saskatchewan

NEW PROVINCE ENTERS
CONFEDERATION UNDER HAPPY
AUSPICES

Regina – Canada is now truly a country from sea to shining seas, two new provinces join the Confederation begun in 1867. On September the first, Saskatchewan and Alberta were carved from the vast lands of the Northwest Territories....

Robert McKenzie pictured in his mind the front page of the September 1905 newspaper written in black and white. That article had made the new province more real than any official Ottawa document that might have come across his desk. The article went on to describe a place forty times the size of Great Britain (population 47 million) with barely 235,000 souls scattered across its rolling flanks, mostly in the southern half. There were even fewer people to the west in the province of Alberta, but the two new members of the Canadian federation now linked the rest of the country from sea to sea – a country of five million people spread across three million square miles from the Atlantic to the Pacific.

Robert recalled it all…

He had been twenty-six years old and working for William Erskine Knowles, federal Minister of Agriculture and the Member of Parliament for Moose Jaw in the newly-minted province of Saskatchewan. There was a land rush out west as thousands of homesteaders claimed their allotted 160 acres of prairie farmland. To secure ownership, they were required to improve the land, grow crops in the field, and build houses and barns. Unless they met those conditions, they would lose title to the acreage. It was a tough life, and homesteaders weren't always punctual in submitting their paperwork, resulting in a backlog in Robert McKenzie's office in Ottawa. When a terse, hand-written note landed on his desk, Robert had worried that his boss was displeased with the delays.

Mr. Knowles requests the attendance of Mr. Robert McKenzie

Knowles was a lawyer as well as a farmer and insisted on first-rate work, so it was with a bit of trepidation that Robert knocked on his door at the appointed time.

"Come in, Robert, come in!" Knowles said as he ushered McKenzie into his oak-paneled office and showed him to one of two leather armchairs in front of a small, brick fireplace. "Excuse the mess, but they've been doing a little renovating." Half of the large room was cordoned off by a long stretch of heavy rope between two stanchions. Behind the rope McKenzie could see a leather settee, two easy chairs, and a meeting table with six chairs partially covered with paint-spattered tarpaulins. He turned back to Knowles, who was lighting a small cigar.

"Want one Robert?" Knowles asked, proffering the box of Coronas.

"No thank you, sir. I don't... Sir, I can explain about the delays in..."

"Never mind that. All done and dusted," Knowles laughed. His hearty demeanor was at odds with his stern countenance, and McKenzie was backfooted for a moment as Knowles continued. "I had Langlois look after it. Simply a matter of lengthening the time allowed for the homesteaders to submit their paperwork. Those sodbusters have a hard enough life and rarely get to town, so we should cut them a little slack, eh? Merely paperwork. Not a problem at all. Which is more than I can say for Holt's bloody Expansion Commission." Knowles waved his cigar around the office. "Look at this! The country's growing faster than a prairie fire with a tailwind. More people need more MPs to represent them in Ottawa, and all those MPs need office space – on that we're all agreed. But rather than build the offices anew, they're subdividing what's already here and doing a damned poor job of it." He puffed furiously on his cigar, filling the room with nutty blue smoke. "They've been at it for two years, and so far, it's been absolute chaos, as you can see around us. But enough about that. How are you getting on?"

"Well enough, sir, but as you say, the demand for Crown land is increasing. I fear we may not be able to keep up with the demand, especially for pre-emptions." Pre-emptions allowed a homesteader to claim an additional 160 acres next door to their original claim, thus doubling their acreage and Robert McKenzie's paperwork.

"Don't I know it. The demand for everything in this country is rapacious. People are itching to get going, to try new things in this new century. Sometimes, I don't see how we can keep up the pace. Still, all our problems should be such happy ones. With that in mind, what would you say to a move out west, eh Robert?"

“Out west, sir?”

“The Territories. Well, Saskatchewan, now. My riding of Moose Jaw.”

“Moose Jaw? Are you sacking me, sir?”

“Sacking you? Hah! No, I’m not sacking you, Robert. Ha ha! The very idea. No, I’m promoting you, if anything. I want you to work in my constituency.”

“Me?”

“I’ve been watching you, Robert. You do the work, you don’t look for shortcuts, and you take the blame when you make a mistake. You’re an honourable man, which is more than I can say for some ‘Honourable Members’ around here, naming no names.” Knowles laughed. Robert may have blushed because he’d seen a few of those men on his own midnight rambles on restless nights, and he felt guilty receiving such praise after behaving like a tomcat while telling Janet he was working late. But Knowles went on. “I need someone I can trust to do the right thing, even when there’s no one looking. Chaps like you are thin on the ground, especially here in Ottawa. Saskatchewan is a full-fledged province now, which means a lot more trade and commerce between the west and Ontario. There’s a hunger to open up this country now that we are truly a nation from sea to sea.”

“What is the job?”

“Asking questions, just like that one. Getting information. Making sure I’m in the loop, as they say. Be my eyes and ears in the riding, Robert. What are the constituents talking about? What are their concerns, their needs? Those homesteaders, for instance. Instead of dealing with some anonymous government agent, they could deal with you to expedite their claims. I'm stuck here in Ottawa for half the year, distracted by all manner of business that has nothing to do with me or Moose Jaw or even Saskatchewan, and by the time I get home, all hell could have broken loose, and I'd never hear about it except at the ballot box. I need somebody I can trust to keep me informed on what's going on with the people I represent, someone who can travel around the riding and take the temperature of the place so that I can represent them here in Ottawa."

"But what would I actually do? I know nothing about running an office, sir."

"You wouldn't run the office, Robert. Norma Hall does all that. Couldn't live without her. But with Norma's help, you'd run my affairs in the riding, be my right-hand man. Like I say, my eyes and ears. You collaborate easily with other people, as I've seen throughout your time in my department. So, you would get to know local farmers, ranchers, businessmen, merchants – find out what they're thinking and let me know."

"Would I move my family out west, too, sir?" MPs only served until the next election, and if Knowles wasn't re-elected in 1908, the job would be short-lived. More importantly, Janet might not appreciate moving 1600 miles away from her family and childhood home to live in a small town way out west with their three young sons, just for the sake of a tenuous, albeit important, position.

"You're thinking the job might not last that long if the voters kick me out in a few years, is that it?" Robert felt like Knowles was reading his mind, but said nothing. "Smart man. Politics is a dodgy business at best. Tell you what – I'll give you a five-year contract, so whatever happens, you'll be good until at least 1910. How does that sound?"

"It's a lot to take in, sir, if you don't mind me saying."

"I do mind you saying 'sir' and would appreciate it if you'd call me Bill if we're to be working more closely together. But you're right, it is a lot to take in. Talk it over with Janet and let me know." Robert was surprised that Knowles even knew Janet's name, much less cared what she thought.

"I must admit to being very intrigued, sir... uh, Bill. I've always wanted to go out west, but Janet may not..."

"...appreciate your young family being uprooted to go live in a small town on the bald prairie?" Knowles laughed. "That's exactly what my Mary Jean said when I suggested we move to the Territories from southern Ontario eight years ago. 'Uncivilized' I think is the way she put it. But unlike here, there's lots of land and houses are inexpensive. You've got a growing family and Saskatchewan has room to grow. Of course, the government will pay to move you out there by train – lock, stock, and chesterfield if you like. And if you are interested in houses with some acreage, I know of a few that are on the market. We could help with the financing if that's required. But it's all up to you."

"I'll talk it over with Janet and let you know by the end of the week. Is that soon enough?"

"Just dandy, Robert."

Alexander was four, Michael three, and Scott had just turned two. In Ottawa, there were good schools, doctors, and recreational and cultural facilities, as well as all the other needs a growing family might have, including family nearby to help in times of trouble. Janet had grown up with two older sisters and her parents, Nathan and Mary Raymer, who owned a small department store in Ottawa. She had dozens of aunts, uncles, and cousins sprinkled around the Ottawa Valley, whereas in Moose Jaw, she wouldn't know a soul. Robert would be busy with his new job, and Janet would be on her own. It wasn't an easy sell, so he was cautious when he broached the subject that night at home.

"Mr. Knowles was talking today about his riding, how vast and varied it is," he began as they did the dishes together after supper. "Did you know that there are 94,000 lakes in Saskatchewan, and the Cypress Hills in the western part of his riding are considered to be the highest point of land between the Rockies and Labrador way down east."

"His riding is called Moose Jaw, is it?" Janet knew full well the name of Knowles' riding and the fact that it was part of the new province of Saskatchewan.

"That's right. Moose Jaw," he said. "There's the city of Moose Jaw, of course, but the riding stretches hundreds of miles from the city itself. Sounds like a splendid area, lots of good land. You know, Saskatchewan just became a province..."

"No! You don't say! Silly man. I do read the newspaper, Robert," Janet laughed. "And why was Mr. Knowles rhapsodizing about his riding?"

"Well, we got talking, and he happened to mention about a position coming up..."

"Yes?"

"...a position coming up in his riding. He suggested..."

"He suggested?"

"Well, he asked if I'd like to..."

"Spell it out, Robert. If you'd like to do what?"

"Manage his riding for him. In Moose Jaw. Saskatchewan." As soon as he said it, Robert heard how ridiculous the whole idea sounded. Go set up housekeeping 1600 miles away in some place where they knew not a single soul? Moose Jaw was just a small town, scarcely a tenth the size of Ottawa. Were there adequate schools for the boys? Proper sanitation and health care? What was he thinking? It was absurd to even consider it.

"What a wonderful idea!" Janet said, throwing her arms around his neck. "This airless Ottawa life will be the death of me otherwise. You're either in or you're not, and everyone is working an angle. And all those receptions you have to attend. Wouldn't be as many of those in Moose Jaw, I'll bet."

Robert was good at meeting and greeting people at such events, but he didn't enjoy it, preferring to sit down and actually discuss ideas with people he met, not just shake their hands and make small talk. But he did his duty, working the rooms representing Knowles and, by extension, the federal Department of Agriculture. At one of those receptions, a fundraiser for some charity he couldn't remember, Robert saw Janet Raymer across the room and fell completely, irrevocably in love. The rest of the evening was a blur. Six years and three kids later, they were well-ensconced in Ottawa society, and now he was proposing that they leave all that behind and move to the wilderness. It was a big ask.

"It'll be a real adjustment," Robert said. "With the kids and..."

"The kids will love it! Just think, all that room to run around. Will there be Indians?"

"As a matter of fact, the Cree have a winter camp just south of Moose Jaw, but..."

"Well, then that's just about perfect. When do we leave?"

While Janet was thrilled with the prospect of moving 'out west,' Robert's mother, Maura, was not.

"What sort of a *sgròbach* place is even called Moose Jaw?" Maura chewed up the Gaelic word for *scruffy* and spat it out like rotten fruit. "Sounds like a trading post. Will there be pelts on your office wall? And what do you call the people there anyway? Moose Jawers?"

"Moose *Javians*, mother. You know, like a play by George Bernard Shaw is called *Shavian*."

"Don't change the subject, Robert. Is Saskatchewan even a province? I thought it was part of those Northwest Territories or something. It's the wilderness, for goodness sake, the back of beyond. Why would you subject yourself and your family to such hardship in the colonies?" When Maura got upset her Scottish burr came roaring back. "Wilderrrrrness." "Harrrrrrdship."

"Saskatchewan became a province just two weeks ago, Mother, as you well know because it was in all the newspapers, and I know you subscribe to the *Ottawa Citizen*," Robert said patiently. "Moose Jaw is a thriving city of more than seven thousand people, with electricity, running water, hospitals, and motor cars. They have an electric railway, which will take you all the way to the southern edge of the city for a nickel. And the city is blessed with several churches." Maura McKenzie insisted her children and grandchildren attend church, so Robert felt that he'd played a trump card. But his mother would not be convinced and put on her Really Serious Face.

"I must tell you, Robert, that there is a much greater incidence of thunderstorms and lightning in that part of the country," she said with conviction. He had no idea how his mother knew this bit of lore, but he felt unable to contradict her. "Your late father would certainly counsel against this move, and I most certainly agree with him." Invoking the ghost of Hamish McKenzie seemed melodramatic and cruel, but Robert kept his powder dry.

"It is an opportunity for me to not only rise in my profession but to acquire land and become a man of means," he said. "Don't you want the best for your son and grandchildren?" Difficult for her to argue with his statements and questions, so his mother switched to emotional blackmail.

"How can you deprive me of my grandchildren?" She almost wept. Almost. "Am I never to see any of you again? How could you be so cruel to your own mother? Are you even thinking of how hard it will be on your children?"

"I *am* thinking of the boys, Mother. I want them to own land, learn how to work it, be self-sufficient, be able to feed people, and become prosperous while doing it. Saskatchewan is a new land, and there's lots of it. I want our boys to grow up where opportunities abound. It is precisely their future I am most concerned about."

But Maura was unmoved. She crossed her arms and looked away, furious that her will would not prevail. Robert knew she would get over it. He'd seen her use this tactic many times, trying to keep his father in line, rest his soul. It didn't work on him either.

Janet's parents were also against their daughter moving 'to the back of beyond' as her father put it.

"What will you do out there with three boys?" Nathan Raymer asked his daughter. "And what will your mother and I do here without them? How can you deprive us of seeing our grandchildren grow up?"

"You can take the train out to visit us, Daddy," Janet said. "And we can come visit you."

"It's one thing to steal my daughter's heart," Nathan said, turning to Robert, "but quite another to steal her and the bairns entirely to live thousands of miles away on the bald prairie."

"Sir, we will be living in a civilized city, and I assure you the prairie is anything but bald." Robert knew Nathan liked maps, so he had brought a new map of what was now western Canada – from Manitoba across the plains of Saskatchewan and Alberta and then over the mountains and down to the sea in British Columbia.

"But where are the cities?" Nathan wanted to know.

"Well, the dots on the map are pretty small right now, I'll grant you, but they'll grow, especially as families like ours move out there and set up our homes and our lives."

"But what about us? What do we do after you've gone out west?" Nathan had a touch of petulance in his voice, and Janet could bite her tongue no longer.

"Papa, I will miss you terribly," she told him. "*We* will miss you terribly. But you have your own life, and we have our own lives. Canada is a young country. We're a young family, and the future for us is out west. Alex, Michael, and Scotty will grow up in a new world where anything is possible."

"But the boys will grow up without their family, Janet. *You'll* grow up without a family, with no links, no kin to help in times of trouble or..."

"This *is* a family, Papa," Janet interrupted. "Look at us. We *are* a family. Robert, me, the boys. And we're moving out west, we're not going to the moon. We hope you'll come out on the train in the summertime for a visit, to see what we see."

Robert and Janet McKenzie and their three young sons moved to Moose Jaw in the spring of 1906 and bought a small farm on the western edge of town. They called it Home Farm because Robert planned to acquire more land beyond its boundaries in the coming years. But Home Farm had everything they needed to get started. There was a barn big enough to stable a few cattle and horses, and there was a large machine shed to house the equipment needed to grow wheat, barley, and hay in the surrounding fields. Over the years, Robert expanded his farming operation by buying nearby land, either from the Crown or from homesteaders who had given up on farming. He spent a lot of time at the Land Titles Building on Fairford Street, poring over maps, deeds, and surveyors' charts to see which parcel of prairie might produce the highest yield.

Moose Jaw was in the middle of Palliser's Triangle, named for the 19th century British explorer John Palliser, who surveyed the land south from the Battlefords and west from Regina to Maple Creek and pronounced the whole area too arid for proper farming. But Robert and others in the area proved him wrong, using dryland farming techniques such as tilling the soil less frequently and leaving an inch or so of stubble after harvest to keep the soil from blowing away during the winter. With a bit of luck, they got good grain crops most years and were able to grow enough hay to feed their livestock. And if a crop failed or the markets dried up, there was always next year.

By 1915, the McKenzie's had built Home Farm into a thriving and diverse operation. If the wheat did badly one year, the cattle operation would pull it through. And there was always next year. Through a mix of unwarranted optimism and an almost fatalistic pragmatism, prairie farmers like Robert McKenzie coaxed a living out of the land some people were calling 'Next Year Country.'

Chapter 3

By 1915, more than fifteen thousand people called Moose Jaw home, and quite a few of them worked for the Canadian Pacific Railway. All day and night at the sprawling railyards along Thunder Creek, trains coupled and uncoupled with resonant metallic clanks as a small army of men made sure the right car got hooked up to the right train on the right set of tracks. Dozens more men worked as conductors, switchers, brakemen, and engineers, driving the trains across the prairie through any kind of weather from hellish heat to arctic cold.

Just across from the railyards, River Street saloons opened early and stayed open late to cater to the shift workers from the yards, as did the brothels and gaming parlours in the nearby houses. The tunnels underneath Main Street that were used to get from the train station to the downtown hotels in poor weather were also used to store contraband such as stolen goods and booze. The US government was threatening the prohibition of alcohol south of the border, so a lot of liquor was being stashed in Canada in anticipation of that legislation. Moose Jaw Police Chief Walter Johnson was a tolerant man who ignored most of the shenanigans as long as he got his cut, something he considered to be a 'sin tax.'

There were many places to atone for all those sins – the big dome of Zion Methodist on Main Street, the spires and stained glass of St Andrew's on Athabasca, or the sturdy brick tower of St Jospeh's Catholic Church over on Third Northwest. As Moose Jaw spread to the north and west, grand houses rose along The Avenues – Grafton, Redland, Clifton, Hall, and Oxford. At least half a dozen schools were sprinkled through the neighbourhoods, including Victoria School on First Avenue East, a two-story, eight-room brick building that was once the only school of its kind on the prairies, long before Saskatchewan became a province.

The three McKenzie boys all attended Victoria School because it was less than a mile from their farm, and they could walk back and forth on all but the coldest days. None of them was a scholar, but they all did the necessary work and got adequate grades. At fourteen, Alexander was a bit of a loner, more interested in machinery than other people. Twelve-year-old Scott was athletic, always going in early or staying late to play rugger or lacrosse. Michael, the middle boy, would rather stay home on the farm than go to school. He had a gentle way with animals and a generous hand when it came to feeding time, one of the reasons they loved him.

Robert McKenzie ran the day-to-day operation of Home Farm, overseeing the seeding, harvest and livestock operations. Janet ran the household and took care of the business side of farming – paying the bills, ordering supplies, and keeping up to date on new ideas. To better understand prairie farming, Janet joined the Women Grain Growers of Saskatchewan and in doing so got to know some of her neighbours, including one woman who could, according to local gossip, divine the future.

Verlane Dupray was opinionated, to be sure. But she was American, so that was to be expected. She came from Baton Rouge, Louisiana, and had a courtly, genteel way of speaking. Some people said she and her husband were run out of Baton Rouge for unspecified offences, but Janet paid no attention to such tittle-tattle and was in fact intrigued by Verlane's ideas. She was a progressive thinker, well-informed with a knowing manner, and a certainty in what she said no matter how controversial it might be. Janet admired that kind of bravery and found Verlane's conversation far more stimulating than that of most women. Their paths crossed one morning in downtown Moose Jaw when they had both stopped to look at a poster plastered onto a telegraph pole.

The image was a cartoon of a young girl tugging at a banner called 'The Vote,' which was being held tenaciously by a young boy.

The caption underneath the cartoon read: "I want the vote, and I mean to have the vote, that's the sort of girl I am." Written on a blank space at the bottom of the poster was the time and location of a meeting the following night to discuss the issue.

"Will you go?" Verlane Dupray asked, raising her dark eyebrows at Janet. "It sounds intriguing, don't you think so? I do believe there may be hope for this country yet." American women were not allowed to vote either, but Verlane thought Canada to be a more civilized country than her own.

"I hadn't really thought...." Janet said. "That is, I'm pretty busy already and..." Politics could be a dangerous subject that inflamed tempers and ruined friendships, so Janet was reluctant to get involved. She liked Verlane Dupray and was afraid of alienating her by saying the wrong thing. She needn't have worried.

"It's only an hour or so," Verlane said. "Could be interesting. Maybe even a barn burner. Unlike the Grain Growers meetings!"

"But I really should..."

"I have a proposal, then." Verlane turned and looked Janet straight in the eye. "I'll pick you up and drop you off. Our stable lad can be our chauffeur in the democrat, and my daughter, Alice, will come along too. She is ten years old and quite keen on women's rights, as am I. Will you join us? It'll be a lovely outing, just us girls."

"How generous," Janet said, seeing no other way out. "Of course I will." They arranged a time for the following evening, and Janet went home, wondering how Robert would feel about her going to a suffragette meeting. She found him in his office engrossed in a monograph on Belgian horses.

"Mrs. Dupray down the road..."

"Mrs. who?" Robert looked up from his reading.

"Dupray. You know. From the Grain Growers?"

"Oh, yes. The Americans. Arthur's wife, I think. Interesting fellow. A lawyer, I believe."

"Yes. They have a daughter, Alice, just a few years younger than Scotty. Well, at any rate, Mrs. Dupray has kindly invited me to..."

"Do I have to go?" Robert had his fill of social functions in Ottawa and attended them in Moose Jaw only if William Erskine Knowles insisted, which he rarely did. Both men felt that politics and business were better done over a cup of coffee or a pasture fence.

"Oh, no. No, this is a meeting for women, to..."

"That's fine, then, fine. But do you need me to give you a ride to this event?"

"Thank you dear, but no. Mrs. Dupray and her daughter will pick me up and bring me back home," Janet said.

"Excellent, then. Dress warmly. It's getting chilly at night. Enjoy yourself, my dear," Robert said, lighting his pipe and going back to his reading, making a mental note to write to Knowles about the burgeoning suffragette movement in Saskatchewan. If they had their way, there would be twice as many voters, and who knew how women would vote on a given subject? Things might get out of hand.

Women had been lobbying for the vote since long before Saskatchewan became a province, but politicians and the newspapers still made light of the issue. One cartoon portrayed Saskatchewan premier Walter Scott making a woman sit up like a dog and beg for the vote. Even some women were opposed to women getting the franchise.

"To my mind their arguments are an attempt at face saving, and a way they have of covering up their botch-work," wrote H. Bate in the *Women and the Grain Growers Guide* in March of 1911. *"They have yet to show me how so-called equal rights will cause the women of today to be able to rear more noble sons than Christ, Luther, Knox, Lincoln, or the great many other honorable and just men who lived in the past."*

Mrs. Bate wasn't alone in her viewpoint. Church groups, temperance thumpers, most schools, many businesses, and almost all corporations were resoundingly opposed to a woman casting a vote. It was not just a political issue but a moral one. If women had the vote, they would want more and yet more rights, all the while neglecting their domestic duties in the kitchens and bedrooms of the land. Everyone got along fine just the way it was, so why tinker with a successful society? But the reality for women was that society was successful only for men. Women took a back seat on most issues and were fed up with the double standard, tired of getting second-class treatment for doing a first-class job.

"When I go out to cast my vote for parliamentary members, as I hope to do in the near future, I shall still go with my family and be treated just as well. Why should I not?" wrote 'A Manitoba Pioneer' in the same issue of the *Guide*.

The following evening at the appointed time, Verlane and Alice drove up to Janet's front door in the four-seat democrat. After they'd wrapped themselves in blankets against the evening chill and set off down the road, Verlane made a prediction.

"March the 14th," she pronounced with confidence. "Tuesday, March the 14th, 1916."

"Your birthday?" Janet asked.

"No, my dear, the vote. That's the day we women will get the vote."

"That's next year. How could you possibly know? Or is it just a guess?" Janet asked, as though the future was an impossible concept. "And the fourteenth? Not a very auspicious number, I shouldn't think."

"Auspicious? Why, my dear, it's Pi Day. Of course, it is auspicious," Verlane said.

"Pie day?" Janet asked. "Why pie day?"

"Pi. A mathematical constant. Three-point-one-four, written as 3/14, hence the connection with March 14th.It's the simplest mathematical expression of Pi, which can run to more than a dozen decimal places."

"I did not know that," Janet said. "Of course, here in Canada, we write March 14 as 14/3, but I understand you do it differently down south."

"Fair point," Verlane allowed, then pressed on. "But auspicious? I'll give you auspicious. The first American town meeting was held in Faneuil Hall in Boston on March 14th; Eli Whitney patented the cotton gin on March 14th, 1794, and March 14th is Albert Einstein's birthday. Is March 14th auspicious? I should say so!"

"But *how* do you know that's when the vote will be allowed? Did somebody tell you? And why that date? March 14th? Where do you... ?" Janet ran out of words.

"Get the information? It's just a... a feeling I guess, Janet. To tell you the truth, I don't really know. And my dear, young Alice here is the same. She sometimes just *knows* a thing that turns out to come true, don't you, my darling? Must be something we both ate!" Verlane laughed and gave Alice a quick hug. They were both small and dark. But while Alice rarely spoke, Verlane was quick with opinions, sharing her ideas about communism, socialism, Darwinism, and religion as well as general comments about the passing parade.

Janet was curious about Alice, about how a child might divine the future or whatever it was that she could do, and what she made of the experience. Janet had never known anyone who would even talk about such things, much less indulge in events and ideas that some academics were calling *paranormal.* But it would be rude to ask the child directly, so Janet kept her counsel and hoped Verlane might elaborate as the carriage clopped along into downtown Moose Jaw.

On Main Street, they climbed down from the democrat and joined dozens of women lined up outside the meeting hall. Inside, almost every seat was already taken, and women stood two and three deep against the walls and at the back of the hall. The clamour of voices was like an aviary, dozens of different species chirping and chatting away together. Janet recognized a few women from the Grain Growers meetings and a few others she'd met while marketing. Michael's Grade Eight English teacher was there, as was the smartly dressed Chinese woman from the grocery store. Murmurs rippled through the crowd as a tall woman in a tweed jacket and mid-calf wool riding skirt stood up on the low stage at one end of the hall and called for quiet.

"It's good to see you all here," she said. Her voice was low-pitched, but while there was no microphone, she could still be heard at the back of the hall. "There are a few women who would like to talk to you this evening. They are just like us – ordinary gals with ordinary lives, but they have something extraordinary to say. It takes great courage for them to speak out tonight because their husbands or their families and friends might disagree with what they have to say and give them a hard time because of it. So please, let's keep it down to a dull roar so we can hear them speak." She stepped down from the dais and was replaced by a stout woman in overalls with her hair tied up in a calico kerchief.

"My name's Annie Faraday, and my old man and me, we run a farm that barely makes money," she began.

"Speak up!" yelled a voice in the crowd.

"Louder," hollered another.

"I'm up before he is," the woman continued, her voice getting stronger and more assured as she spoke. "I get the day going, scatter feed to the chickens, get the wood in, and start the fire in the stove. Then I make breakfast and clean up after. We both work all day, every day, to keep the place going, only his day ends after evening milking when he bellies up to the supper table while I've still got a few hours to put in cleaning up and getting ready for the next day. He gets all the money, and he gets to vote, ya see? Me? I have to ask for pocket change and have no say in any of the farming decisions or even in household matters. Is that fair? I'd say it's not. I just want equal treatment. Thank you." She stepped back a few paces and then turned and left the stage as the women in the crowd cheered and applauded.

It wasn't just farm wives demanding equal say in how things were run. The smartly dressed woman from the grocery store got up in front of the crowd and spoke in a clear, no-nonsense voice.

"You all know me. I'm Maude Chang, and I know a lot of you shop at my husband's grocery store. I work there all day doing the store's accounts and running the till, then when I come home, I have to work some more to feed my family and do all the chores, like laundry, ironing, mending, and cleaning, that keep the household running smoothly. I do all that on the weekend, too, while my husband reads the paper and waits for supper. I do two jobs when most of the men I know only do one. Equality's not too much to ask. Damn right, I want the vote."

A whoop went up as the applause began. Women stood up, cheered, clapped, stamped their feet, and some even whistled.

"Damn right, I want the vote!" called a middle-aged woman from the middle of the crowd.

"Damn right, I want the vote!" said a small, older woman with a surprisingly large voice.

"Damn right, I want the vote! Damn right, I want the vote!" The meeting room echoed with the chant until there was a pounding on the door.

When someone opened the door, a tall, thin woman in spectacles hissed, "Ladies, ladies, ladies, there's a little girls' dance class in the adjoining room.   Kindly behave yourselves." She turned on her heel and clip-clopped back down the hall in high dudgeon. The door was quickly closed, and laughter rippled through the crowd.   When it subsided, everyone hugged each other. After cleaning up the room and putting away the chairs, they quietly left. Outside their breath was frosty on the October night air as they talked about what they'd seen and heard.

"I thought the speakers were very brave," Janet said. "I'm not sure I'd feel as bold if I had to get up in front of such an assembly."

"I agree," said Verlane as they got into the democrat and wrapped the big rugs around their knees and ankles. "And they may get an earful from their husbands when they get home. It takes a lot of guts to be the tall poppy and risk getting your head sliced off."

Janet was slightly disturbed by the imagery but kept her counsel as Alice spoke up.

"Mom, why did that woman say that she was sick of the campaign to give women the vote?" The audience had booed and cat-called when the remark was made, and Alice wasn't sure what she should be feeling. Saskatchewan women had been asking for the vote since before she was born, so she'd grown up listening to debates around their dining room table about equal rights, and she saw first-hand the stress that such discussions put on friendships and marriages, even her parents'. Voices were often raised, arms were crossed, and the air grew hot and then very cold. The next morning at breakfast, a frosty silence would prevail. Over the years, a *détente* evolved, where Arthur allowed that maybe women could vote, and Verlane could see that perhaps giving women more rights could cut into what were now, at least, some men's rights. Now, she tried to explain the concept of trade-offs so that her ten-year-old daughter could understand.

"It's just hard for some people to fight all the time," Verlane said. "Sometimes they need a break. Not a win, necessarily. Just a break from the constant battle. Life's hard enough already, Alice. Did you hear the weariness in her voice? People only have so much fight in them, and they sometimes have to save it for themselves. We have to respect that. We can't belittle them when they are battle-weary."

"But the goal is so close, so why wouldn't she fight even harder to get it done? You always say, when you're going through hell, keep going."

"That's my girl, using my words against me," Verlane laughed. "May you always have the energy to fight for what you want and the wisdom to know when to stop."

"Do you still stand by your prediction, Verlane?" Janet asked with a twinkle in her eye.

"After what I saw in there, I am even more certain. It's so apparent that it won't be necessary to implement the Lysistrata Option to change men's minds," Verlane said.

"Lisa who?" Alice asked.

"Don't they teach you anything in school?" Verlane asked. "Lysistrata. Look her up in the encyclopedia when we get home, then you'll remember it better than if I tell you."

The Supreme Court of Canada would not declare that women were 'persons' until 1929. Even so, women in Saskatchewan were the first in Canada to get the vote, by official decree on Tuesday, March 14, 1916, just as Verlane Dupray had foretold, thus cementing her reputation as a woman with 'the gift.'

Chapter 4

It was still dark, and the morning air shimmered with ice crystals as Michael went outside to feed the animals. The new snow squeaked under his boots, and the landscape looked like a photographic negative – the ground stark white and the bushes and trees all shades of grey and black. He couldn't tell how much snow had fallen overnight because the wind had sculpted drifts like whipped meringue around the trees and up against the house and barn. Alex had been out earlier to shovel the steps and the path to the barn, carving pathways through what looked like a foot of snow in some spots. Alex was always up and doing before everyone else, ready for another long day after only four or five hours of sleep. By the time Michael got outside, the wind had died down to almost nothing, and although it was below zero, he wasn't cold. Winter made him feel alive, vital, and ready to do whatever needed doing. And he enjoyed taking care of animals.

"Don't forget that extra meal for the new heifer," his father had reminded him while Michael was bundling up to go outside.

"She's growing fast, so let's keep her happy and healthy."

Michael didn't need to be reminded. The calf had been born a month early, and for a few weeks, they feared the tiny creature wouldn't make it through the February cold spell. It was Michael who made sure she latched on right from the start to get that vital colostrum that only comes from mother's milk, and it was Michael who brought the calf inside on nights when it was too cold in the barn and sat with her on the floor of the summer kitchen with a fire in the cookstove.

"Can I have a calf for 4-H?" Michael asked his father. 4-H Clubs were a new idea brought up from Ohio that year to encourage kids to excel at farm-related projects such as livestock rearing.

"You want *a* calf?" Robert asked him. "Or you want *that* calf?"

"Well, *that* calf is pretty healthy, and I have been taking care of her right from the start almost." Michael had a natural way with animals. They accepted him as one of their own, and maybe he was.

"Are you going to give her a name?" Robert knew that kids had a habit of getting attached to any creature they named, and there was a need in the cattle business for a certain dispassionate toughness when it came time to sell or butcher livestock.

"No, sir. She'll just be MK74, like on her ear tag." The McKenzies were a modern farming family, and Robert was one of the first to adopt the ear tag system developed in 1913 as a way to track tuberculosis in cattle. There was a chart in the barn and another in Robert's office upstairs, detailing each animal's growth and development.

"Then yes," said Robert. "She's yours until she's sold at the fall fair. Make sure you register her with the 4-H Club right away, though. There may be a deadline. I've heard they're sticklers for following the rules."

"Yes, sir!" Michael said. He would write to the 4-H Club that very morning before he left for school and leave the letter to be picked up from the mailbox at the end of the driveway. Meanwhile, the animals were hungry. The calf in question was already bawling for her breakfast, poking her pink nose through the rails of the stable. Michael dipped a five-gallon pail into the box containing the calf starter mix and carried it over to MK74.

"You and me," Michael said as he poured some of the mixture into her feeding trough. "We're gonna show 'em what a prize-winning heifer looks like, aren't we?" She gobbled up the meal as he rubbed her bristly forehead, then he forked a swatch of hay into her stall and went around doing the same for the other half-dozen cattle and horses.

The Downy woodpecker had been at the suet hung from a low branch of a cottonwood tree behind the barn, but overnight, the block of fat and seed had frozen so solid that not even the Downy's hard, short bill could penetrate it. Michael swapped out the suet with a softer cake brought from inside the house and poured two kilos of sunflower seeds into the feeder. Within seconds, the chickadees were there, then a group of purple finches, followed by squadrons of sparrows swooping in from their various roosts around the area. A fat squirrel scampered up the cottonwood to get at the feeder, and the birds scattered briefly, then fluttered in again to share in the bounty. Michael watched them for a moment, then went inside for breakfast.

The year 1917 was starting out rather well for Michael McKenzie. He was fifteen years old, his grades were good for a change, and now he had a calf to raise on his own. He would show his father what kind of cattleman he could be. He was a fair student at school, but his heart was on the farm. He couldn't wait for the afternoon bell to ring so he could walk home and start in on his chores. Chores? They weren't chores at all. He loved working with the livestock and didn't even mind cleaning up after them. Cattle, horses, even the excitable chickens were calm and tractable around him, and he handled them with ease. While he fed the animals, he thought about what he would do with the quarter section of land he knew would be his one day. After breakfast, he put the 4-H letter and his schoolbooks in a saddle bag which he slung over his shoulder.

"You coming Scotty?" he hollered upstairs. Before they left for school, he and Scott would let all the animals out for the day into the fenced pasture behind the barn. Alex had gone to school earlier to study for a math test.

"Yeah, yeah, I'm coming," Scott said, tumbling down the stairs. "We still got lots of time." He had an internal clock that allowed him to know the exact time of day or night. It was uncanny. Also annoying.

"Do you have your toque on, Scott?" Janet asked from the kitchen.

"Yes, Mom," Alex said, rolling his eyes at Michael. He was 14 years old, but to his mother, he would always be the baby of the family.

"Bye, Mom," they chorused. "Bye, Dad." Robert hollered goodbye from upstairs in his office where he was cooking up some horse-trading deal.

The two boys walked to the barn and went down each aisle of stalls opening the gates. It took the animals a moment to realize they were free to walk out of the barn and into the wider world. The two cows, who had yet to calve that spring, were particularly slow and would have been happy to spend the whole day inside the warm barn, so Michael and Scott had to whoop and whistle to get them moving.

Clouds, the colour of bruised eggplant, hung low over the small winter pasture as the cattle and horses meandered around and pawed at the snow to see if there was any grass to be had. Then Major whinnied, tossed his mane, and galloped off toward the far fence, where he turned hard, throwing up a spray of turf and snow before charging back. Scott quickly closed the pasture gate and turned to Michael.

"Is he OK?" Scott asked. Michael was the family expert on animals. Even their father said so.

"I don't think so," Michael said as the stallion stamped and snorted, spooking the other horses. The cattle shuffled away from the commotion and resumed pawing at the snow.

"What is it boys," asked their father, putting on his coat as he came out of the house. He'd been watching from his office window as Major began stirring up trouble and rushed downstairs to see what the problem was.

"Major's kinda spooked," said Michael. As if on cue, the horse reared on his hind legs and whinnied, his front hooves pawing the air, and his eyes wild and staring. As soon as his front feet touched the ground, Major thundered off across the snowy pasture again, zig-zagging this way and that as if trying to elude some unseen foe.

"Major," Robert called out, standing on the lower fence rail. "Major! Easy boy.

Come on back here, big fella!" The horse ignored him, chewing up the snowy ground with his hooves as he trotted back and forth impatiently while shaking his big shaggy head. The other four horses had retreated to the gate, hoping to be let out so they could get away from this crazy animal. Even the cattle were lowing, their slow bovine brains unsure what was going on but upset just the same.

Far across the pasture, a small, electric-blue light grew larger and glowed ever brighter, hovering just above the snowy ground as it came toward them. It put Robert in mind of an angel about to appear in some Sunday School story. He and the two boys stared at the sight, and even Major calmed down for a moment to take in this luminous tumbleweed of energy crackling and hissing toward them over the snow. Above them, the sky lowered almost to the ground as if the gods themselves were frowning. Then, the world took a collective gasp and held its breath for a long moment. The air was slashed by a snapping blue light which burst brightly for a split second then dimmed and vanished like it never existed. The wind died to nothing, the earth exhaled, and big fat flakes of snow began to fall through the electric air.

Major nickered, shook his head, and stamped his front right hoof indignantly as if to say I told you so, then trotted off a few paces to paw the ground in search of grass like the rest of the stock as if nothing had happened. Bewildered, Robert gazed at the scene for a few moments, then looked at his two astonished boys.

"Let's go in the house," he said quietly. "I think perhaps school is cancelled for today."

"Will Alex be okay at school?" Scott asked once they were inside and taking off their boots and coats.

"I'm sure he will, Scotty," Robert said, not sure at all. "It was likely just localized lightning here on the farm, although I can't say I've ever seen lightning in the wintertime."

"I think I know what that was," Michael said. "The Cree call it Thundersnow."

"How do you know what the Cree call it, son?"

"They told me."

"Who told you?"

"The Cree, sir. On the river. We were fishing and got to talking."

"You shouldn't be down there on your own, Michael," Robert said. "For one thing, that's their place, not ours." The nomadic Cree camped at the confluence of Thunder Creek and the Moose Jaw River, where they fished and hunted through the winter. It was a peaceful camp for the most part. They had little interaction with the townspeople, and Robert thought things should stay that way, especially where his children were concerned.

"But they invited me," Michael said.

"Invited you? Who invited you?"

"A fella in my class. Johnny Deerfoot."

"He's Cree?" Most Cree children went to the residential schools in Regina or Lebret that were set up by the federal government, the Grey Nuns, and other religious orders. Robert didn't agree with the way the Indian kids were forced to go to the government boarding schools, but he was sure that some of them at least were better fed and housed at the school than at home. The Cree were a nomadic people, and separating children from their parents was never a good idea, no matter how noble the motives. Robert felt they should be left alone to roam the prairies as they always had, camp where they'd always camped, eat what they'd always eaten, and speak the language they'd always spoken. Even with homesteaders claiming some of the land, there was plenty of room for everyone in Saskatchewan.

"No, sir, he's not Cree. He's... can I say it?"

"Say what?"

"A half-breed sir. Johnny says it's a mean thing to say."

"And he's right, son," said Robert. "It is mean. He's just a boy like you, with a mom and a dad. Now you say he took you down to their camp?"

"Yes, sir. His father's Cree, but his mom ain't... uh, isn't. So Johnny goes to visit his dad at the camp sometimes, and he invited me to go too because I said I liked fishing." He and Johnny had walked the short distance from the school down to the river and then southwest along the bank to where the smell of woodsmoke and fish and frybread sweetened the air. Dogs and kids ran free around the camp while the adults talked and smoked. Sometimes, a jug was passed around.

"And did you catch anything?"

"Yes, sir, we caught three pike, except they call them *kinosêw*, I think."

"You didn't bring any home?" Robert asked, raising his eyebrows.

"We gave them to his dad, sir, because they have a pretty big family to feed, and I figured we were okay."

"Good boy," said Robert. "But what about this thundersnow?"

"They say it follows people," Michael said.

"Follows people? How?"

"Like it's attracted to them."

"And you believe this, son?"

"No, sir, but they do."

"Alright, enough about thundersnow. Off you go now and see if your mother needs any help with chores around the house. Then you can do a little reading ahead for school. And this afternoon, we need some of that pine split for the furnace. Otherwise, the day is yours."

Robert returned to his office but found it difficult to concentrate on the documents Knowles had sent for him to consider because his mind kept returning to the notion of thundersnow. Wasn't lightning a creature of heat? Whoever heard of lightning when there was snow on the ground? Yet, he saw it with his own eyes. Did this episode of thundersnow mean that the superstitions were true? Did lightning strike the firstborn, and, if so, were he and Alexander at risk? Could the McKenzie Curse be true? Was there malevolence afoot, some elemental retribution for past sins? Or was it just some freakish phenomenon of the tempestuous Saskatchewan climate? Too many questions without answers blurred in his brain. He tried to dismiss them, but like a wheel in a snowy rut, he kept returning to thundersnow.

Chapter 5

Pack up your troubles in your old kit bag. And smile, smile, smile. While you've a lucifer to light your fag, smile, boys, that's the style..."

George Price was certainly ready to pack up his old kit bag and go home as soon as the war was over, which, according to scuttlebutt, might be any day now. Well, he wouldn't go home to Cape Breton, where he grew up poor and hungry. Home now was Moose Jaw, Saskatchewan, a thriving young city in a younger province, where anything was possible. Sure, he was just a farm labourer now, but he was learning the business of agriculture, and one day he would get a job as a grain inspector or maybe open a feed store.

He was 25 years old in the summer of 1917, when the Military Service Act became law. Within a few months, George was off the farm and in uniform, trained, and on his way to fight with the Canadian Expeditionary Force in Europe. He'd been in the trenches for just over a year, but it seemed like forever. The bad food, the mud, and the hours of boredom were followed by harrowing stretches of withering fire from an unseen enemy and horrible, unspeakable wounds among his comrades. And now that it was almost over, he'd have to think about getting a job again, as if he could just go back to normal after all he'd seen. Life was strange.

"What's it like puttin' in windows, Art?" George asked the man crouched next to him in the foxhole. Art Goodmurphy was a glazier in Regina when he wasn't hunkered down with the Saskatchewan Battalion in Ville-sur-Haine, just outside Mons in southern Belgium. It was getting colder as the morning went on, as if someone forgot to light the world's furnace, and both men were huddled over a small Primus stove, rubbing their gloved hands together to keep warm.

"Cut yer hands a lot," Art said. He pulled off his right glove and showed George the lattice of tiny scars on the hardened palms of his hand from handling large panes of glass. "Ya wear thick gloves, but the glass'll cut right through 'em, see? Even leather."

"I get the same thing with bob wire," George said. "Musta strung fifty miles of the stuff and it rips right through everything. Mustn't grumble, though. I'druther be stringin' bob wire than sittin' here, much as I enjoy yer company, Art." George figured that was just the way of it, though. Working men everywhere had to put up with the cuts and scrapes and bumps and bruises that came with any job.

"Well, guess we'll be back at work soon enough though, eh?" Art pulled out his tobacco pouch and rolled a cigarette, then passed the pouch and papers to George. "Captain said they figure today or tomorrow they could sign the peace treaty. Hope they do it soon." They both smoked in silence for a bit, wrapped up in their own private thoughts of being home after the war.

Neither man was a professional soldier. They'd been hastily trained to replace the troops that had fallen in their thousands at the Somme, Passchendaele, Vimy, and Ypres, which they called Wipers. And now, here they were in another trench near another small European town, just killing time until the war was over. George didn't hear the crack of the German sniper's rifle because before the sound could reach his ears, the bullet had severed his spine. He was dead as he fell into Art Goodmurphy's arms. It was two minutes before 11 am on Monday, November 11, 1918, and George Price was the last Commonwealth soldier to die in the war to end all wars.

Such a terrible tragedy, Janet McKenzie thought as she read the story in the *Times Morning Herald*. Such a waste of a life to wait for an arbitrary time such as 11 am to stop killing people. Why not at midnight the night before? Why not as soon as the peace treaty was signed? Or maybe even before going to war in the first place. How many young men like George Price had to die unnecessarily?

Janet was thankful that her own sons weren't quite old enough for military service. Alexander, the oldest, had just turned 17, and at 36, her husband Robert was almost too old. At any rate, he was considered an essential worker on the home front and not eligible for conscription. Janet had been helping with the various charities and drives that had been held during the war years, but even that sense of urgency was worlds away from the horrors of the fighting in Europe. Two hundred Moose Jaw boys died over there, including poor George Price. Most people knew someone who had lost a son.

And now this horrid Spanish flu, which some said was brought home by returning soldiers. It took Maura McKenzie's life in the summer of 1918 when she was barely sixty. All train travel had been suspended because of the war and the fear of spreading the flu, so Robert could not attend his mother's funeral or see where she was laid to rest. By the time it abated in 1920, the Spanish flu epidemic had killed more than fifty thousand Canadians, most of them between the ages of twenty and forty. Five thousand people died in Saskatchewan alone, almost as many as the province had lost in the war. It seemed particularly cruel to inflict such pain and suffering just when life was supposed to be getting better.

The McKenzie family had kept to themselves as much as they could during the epidemic, and they all came through the worst of it alright. Scott got sick in September along with most of his rugby teammates, but it was a mild bout and he recovered quickly. Now Janet could turn her full attention to ensuring her three sons finished their education and were well-prepared for a life that she hoped would never include going to war. She even dared to hope that one or two of her boys would follow their father into farming. It was an honest way to make a living, and they could do some good in the world by feeding people.

"No man is rich unless he owns property," Robert was fond of saying. He'd been quite canny in buying and selling property since they arrived in Moose Jaw. He knew the Land Grants of Western Canada program inside out and was able to capitalize on some inside knowledge to acquire good land at low prices. He bought each of his sons 160 acres and farmed the land himself until they were of an age to take it on.

Robert no longer worked for William Erskine Knowles or the federal government. Knowles made a successful move to provincial politics in June of 1918, and while McKenzie helped out with the transition, he declined the full-time job as Knowles' aide.

A dozen years in the world of politics was a lifetime. There were too many meetings, too many nights away from home, and he was happy to turn his attention back to ranching, farming, and especially breeding horses.

Over several months, he had corresponded with Walter H. Hanley of Providence, Rhode Island and had finally settled on buying a pair of horses from the breeder. The most complicated part of the negotiations was the means by which the animals would be shipped to Saskatchewan, after the war was over and travel restrictions had been lifted. Hanley promised to delegate one of his top trainers to accompany the horses on their two-thousand-mile journey and so the deal was struck.

The pair of bay Belgians arrived in Moose Jaw by rail from Rhode Island by way of Montreal and Toronto in May of 1919. A crowd gathered as the train pulled in, and the magnificent horses were led down a ramp from their special car. It was the first time most people had seen such giant draft horses with their shaggy manes, brawny backs and shoulders, sturdy legs, and massive feathered hooves. The two horses were being managed by a ruddy-cheeked man in a tweed suit. Robert stepped forward and extended his hand as the horses stood quietly.

"Mr. Henry Bragg, I presume. I am Robert McKenzie. Welcome to Moose Jaw."

"Thank you, sir. Henry Bragg at your service. And these two beauties are Cleo and Caesar," said the man in tweed, patting the nose of each horse in turn. "It has been my pleasure to accompany them from Providence, and I am happy to say they have behaved perfectly and are in sound health."

"I am pleased to hear it, sir," Robert said. "I don't believe I have ever seen such a fine-looking brace of animals in all my life."

"These are two of Mr. Hanley's favourites," Bragg said. "And I must confess, two of my own favourites as well."

"They look in tip-top shape, considering it's been such a long journey," Robert said. Indeed, the horses' coats appeared shiny in the warm spring sunshine.

"And they're better-tempered than most folk I know," Bragg laughed. "Never a spot of trouble with either of them, and I'm going to miss them."

"I hope you'll stay with us for a time before you make your way back to Rhode Island," Robert said. He knew Michael would especially like to meet this American horse trainer and perhaps learn a thing or two from him.

"Thank you, sir, I would be delighted. A few more days in their company would not go amiss, I should say."

Bragg stayed at Home Farm for a month, discussing with Robert the finer points of breeding and caring for the Belgians. The two men often went for rides in the countryside on Robert's quarter horses. Bragg enjoyed the wide-open spaces and endless skies, and Robert would have been happy to hire him as a farm manager, but duty called. On a fine morning in late June, Henry Bragg boarded the train heading back east.

"You must come back and visit them anytime, Mr. Bragg," McKenzie said as he waved goodbye. "You'd be most welcome."

"I may just take you up on that, Robert," Bragg said as the train pulled out of the station.

Cleo and Caesar were all that Robert hoped they would be. They could pull anything with a yoke and took the blue ribbon in every exhibition they entered. But their real value was as blood stock. Cleo had just turned three and was old enough to breed. Caesar was up to the task and within the year a foal called Duke was cantering around the pasture behind his mother through the early summer of 1920. The rains were good that spring and the grass was lush. But the first cutting of hay was all there would be. July was hot and dry, the grass turned brown, wheat stalks withered, and the ground was harder than a macadam road. Not a drop of rain fell from late June until a day in early September, when the skies darkened and the intoxicating smell of ozone filled the air.

"C'mon, help me get the stock in," Robert shouted to Michael over the wind as they watched the approaching storm. "You get those other horses, and I'll take care of the Belgians." It was impossible to tell what havoc a summer storm could wreak, but it was smart to get out of its way.

Michael grabbed a bucket of oats and, like the Pied Piper of Moose Jaw, enticed the seven stock horses from the paddock into the stables with the promise of treats. Robert took Cleo's bridle and led her into the barn, with Duke trotting happily behind. Once they were in their stalls and given nosebags full of oats, Robert went back for Caesar, who was acting uncharacteristically skittish.

"Come on now, old son, let's get out of this weather," he said as he walked slowly up to Caesar and took hold of his bridle. The big horse nickered and shied as a flash of lightning arced across the valley.

"Steady now, fella," Robert said, trying to retain his grip on Caesar's bridle. "Easy now."

Another flash crackled up in the clouds, and Caesar whinnied and reared. Robert let go of the bridle and stepped back out of the way of those massive hooves. The horse bolted for the far fence of the paddock and looked as if he might jump over it but stopped short and turned back in a cloud of dust. Eyes wild, Caesar galloped straight toward Robert as if the hounds of hell were on his trail, then froze mid-stride as the thunderbolt struck. His mane and tail stood on end, his knees buckled, and the great horse gave one final agonized cry as he tumbled to the ground before McKenzie's horrified eyes. Electricity hung in the air as a sing-song memory threaded through Robert's head:

"Spare the rod and share the blame. Watch the world go up in flames. Your protection or your shame. Take the rod, and fire's tamed. *In tuo capite fiat.* On your head be it."

Should he have taken heed after Major was spooked by lightning a few years back? Was that an omen, a warning to keep his livestock out of harm's way? But who believes in omens? And how would a lightning rod on the house have attracted the bolt away from Caesar in the paddock? It seemed particularly cruel to take his favourite horse, the apple of his eye. Why Caesar and not any of the dozen other creatures in the pasture? It seemed as though Caesar was a particular target. And if lightning could take his favourite horse, why not his eldest son, Alexander? It had killed Robert's father, also a firstborn. A shiver ran down Robert's spine with the realization that he too was a firstborn. Was the McKenzie Curse true and, if so, how could he counter it? How could he protect his son from the fate that befell his father? He tried to put the thoughts out of his mind but a pervading sense of dread would not leave him alone.

Chapter 6

There were more than sixty thousand motor vehicles in Saskatchewan, and Alexander McKenzie was going to learn how to service each and every one of them. Ownership of private automobiles in 1922 was growing faster in Saskatchewan than anywhere else in the young country of Canada. Perhaps the vast distances between prairie towns, or the fact that, unlike Central Canada, passenger rail service in Saskatchewan was spotty and slow and always had to give the right of way to freight. Or maybe the people who chose to live on the prairies were independent and wanted a means of transportation that suited their needs and personal timetables. Whatever the reason, Alexander would be ready to take care of all their mechanical needs. He was particularly interested in farm machinery because there would always be a need for food and for people to fix the machines that plant and harvest the food.

In school Alex loved math, admired the precision and exactitude required to solve complex problems. He liked the idea that math was immutable. One plus one would always be two, and you could always get from here to there. For Alex, mechanics was simply the physical manifestation of mathematics. Since he was eight or nine, he'd been helping his father repair their various pieces of equipment – the combine, seeder, baler, and the Fordson Model F tractor that was the workhorse of the farm. He instinctively knew how a particular machine should function and was particularly good at improvising in the field when a piece of equipment broke down. Nearby farmers often called on Alex to give them a hand with breakdowns, and he never said no, which is how he found himself on his back under a combine harvester in Andy O'Kane's field on one of the hottest days of the year.

"I just can't get the blades to engage," Andy said.

"Could be your power take-off, maybe," Alex said as he scooted around under the machine. The combine had stopped mid-swath and the bruised and half-cut wheat stalks tickled his back and smelled of unleavened bread.

"Damn thing's only ten years old," Andy said. "Fella sold it to me said it'd last longer'n I would."

"It's still in good shape but when did you last clean under here, Andy?" Alex laughed as he pulled stalks of barley and oats from the machinery. "I think we got samples of crops from two or three years back."

"Oh, I can't get under there anymore; you know that, Alex! Crawling around down there's for youngsters like yourself, not for some stiff old geezer like me. And like I say, the fella said it'd last a lifetime."

"Hand me that belt, will you?" Alex reached out his hand from under the combine and pointed to his pile of tools and parts laid out on an oil cloth next to the combine. Andy passed him the belt, and there was some clanking and banging for a few moments before Alex wriggled out from under the machine and stood up. "Try 'er now," he said.

Andy clambered up into the combine's cab and pushed the starter. The exhaust stack belched black smoke that turned a misty gray as the engine settled into a throaty purr. As he drove the machine forward, he engaged the cutting blades, which turned as they should. He disengaged the blades, stopped the machine for a moment, and hollered down from the cab.

"What did ya do?"

"It was your power take-off belt, like I said," Alex hollered back. "Just a little bit worn and slipping. Be gentle when you engage the PTO, and the new belt'll wear in over the next few hours."

"I'm much obliged, Alex. We're burnin' daylight, so I better get back to cutting this wheat, but send me your bill, OK?"

"No charge, sir. Easy fix."

"You'll go hungry with that approach," Andy called with a wave as the combine rolled away across the field.

Alex didn't need the money. Not yet. He was twenty-one, unmarried, with a full-time job keeping the machinery running at Home Farm. He wasn't interested in farming his 160-acre piece of Saskatchewan just yet, so he leased it nominally to his father, but actually to his younger brother Michael, who this year was growing malting barley for a brewery in Regina. Their father, Robert, had stepped back from much of the day-to-day farm work to concentrate on his breeding program for the horses and cattle. Michael handled most of the actual farming but didn't have much of an aptitude for machines, so Alex ensured that the tractor, combine, seeder, and other equipment were running properly. He worked. He ate. He slept badly. The work kept him from thinking about what happened three summers earlier, and what he might have done to prevent it.

In August of 1919, Alex and three friends from high school climbed into his rebuilt 1911 Model T and headed west along a rutted road once known as the Red Deer Trail. Alex had modified the car by beefing up the suspension and putting bigger tires on it, but it was still a bumpy couple of hours on a bad road before they arrived at a well-shaded spot on Sandy Creek, where the water pooled and there was good fishing. The Cree had camped there forever, leaving behind stone tools, bones, and firepits.

Tommy Armstrong helped Alex set up the two tents while Wilf Simpson and Carl Spinetti went looking for firewood. All four boys had camped there before and knew the terrain well. Carl was the fisherman of the bunch and in half an hour had pulled two fat brook trout out of the pool and had them cleaned and ready for the grill.

"Hey guys, let's see if we can pick up some music," Wilf said after they'd eaten. He had brought along his latest project, something he called a 'portable' radio. It was as heavy as a building brick, largely because of the big black battery that powered it.

"There's no radio stations out here, Wilf," Tommy said with a chuckle. "We can barely pick up the one in town on our big Crosley in the living room, and it's got an antenna on the roof."

"This one has an antenna, too. See?" Wilf flipped up a small square wire gadget and twiddled the radio's dial. "Bet we could pick up Chicago."

"Yeah, right," scoffed Tommy. "I'd bet a buck you can't."

"No bet," said Wilf as an ethereal voice came through the little speaker.

"This is KYW, Chicago, presenting an evening of dance music for your listening pleasure."

Music crackled out of the radio, fading in and out like a broadcast from another time.

"How do you do that?" Tommy asked.

"It's magic," Wilf said. "I'm a crafty magician."

"Git outta here," Tommy scoffed. "What's the trick?"

"Sky wave propagation," said Wilf. "They call it skip. At night, radio waves bounce off the ionosphere, so they can sometimes travel thousands of miles. A guy at school showed me how it works."

The stars came out, the music faded, and the fire died. Tommy sloshed some water and dirt on the embers, and they all got into their sleeping bags. Alex shared a tent with Wilf, who kept trying to tune in more stations on his radio.

"Can you please turn that off so we can get some sleep?" Alex asked.

"Aw, this is the best time to do it, after midnight," Wilf pleaded.

"Well, take it outside then," Alex said.

Wilf grudgingly took his radio and sleeping bag outside and sat by the fire circle, searching for distant radio stations.

Alex awoke to a sharp crack, followed by the splat of raindrops on the canvas tent. He sat up and saw that Wilf wasn't in the tent, so he poked his head outside the flap to see him sitting by the firepit's circle of stones, cradling his radio. Smoke rose from his cindered body as raindrops hissed on the metal box holding the radio. Alex scrambled out of the tent and ran to Wilf but then stopped short as he heard the crackling buzz around the body. Carl and Tommy emerged from their tents and stared wild-eyed and speechless at the sight of their smoldering friend.

Years had passed since that fateful camping trip, but Alex had never forgiven himself for sending Wilf to his death by lightning. No amount of commiserating or consoling from his family or friends could heal the hole in his soul. Alex was certain that the lightning was meant for him, as a firstborn McKenzie, and should have struck the tent and killed him rather than poor Wilf, who Alex had kicked out of the tent. His dreams were haunted by a smiling Wilf Simpson, smoldering and fiddling with his radio, tuning in nothing but screams. Alex withdrew from social contact and concentrated on his work, routinely putting in 12-hour days servicing the machinery at Home Farm or out in some neighbour's field.

Visits like this one to O'Kane's farm were an education for Alex, as well as a kind of advertising. He was certain that when farmers knew they could trust him to fix their broken machines, the word would get around, and he'd be in business. With a brick-and-mortar service station, he could then start charging real money for his services. And with a few extra staff, he could offer to do repairs in the field. He had his eye on a building in town that would make an ideal garage. It was on a back street with empty lots all around it, like someone had left it there and forgotten all about it. There was even room to park cars waiting for service. It was a perfect situation.

While he was looking over the property, a small dark man and a horse-drawn cart came slowly down the alley.

The cartwheels squeaked in time to a little rhyme the man repeated in a sing-song voice.

"Spare the rod and share the blame. Watch the world go up in flames. Your protection or your shame. Take the rod and fire's tamed." A hand-painted sign on the side of the cart read:

THORSON LIGHTNING RODS

The man led his horse and cart to where Alex was standing, looked straight at him, and stuck out his hand to shake.

"Thorson's the name," he said. "Lightning's the game."

"Uh, OK, hi. I'm Alex," shaking the man's hand, which was small but hard and callused.

"If this place you are buying, a rod you'll be trying," Thorson said.

"Rod?"

"A lightning rod to save your life. Diverting trouble, fire, and strife."

"Look, I don't even..."

"Firstborn you are. There is no doubt that lightning always seeks you out."

"Look, I don't know about that, but I haven't even decided whether I'll buy this place yet. It may not even be for sale. There's no sign."

"Buy it, you will. I know for a fact. Lightning will kill if a rod you do lack."

Alexander gave an involuntary shiver, remembering his father talking about seeing his own father struck by lightning. Could his grandfather's life have been saved if he had a lightning rod on his roof? They were cheap enough and might actually work.

The man's lilting voice was hypnotic, so Alex tried to disengage from the conversation and get back to looking over the property. He'd heard about the Travellers and others who talked people into a trance and then stole their jewelry and other valuables. He didn't necessarily believe the stories, but he didn't want to continue talking to this man either. He wanted to find out who owned the property and make them an offer.

"OK, give me your card, and I'll get in touch if I do decide to buy this place," Alex said, hoping to send the man on his way.

"No card. No phone. I work alone. I'll find you when the time is right. The rod protects you day and night." And with that, Thorson led his horse and cart down the alley, his rhyming voice fading as the cartwheels squeaked.

The encounter unsettled Alex, and he paced back and forth, uncertainly, for some time in front of the property, wondering if the little man was a jinx. Then he put that thought out of his mind and, instead, visualized the building full of mechanics working all day long, keeping Moose Jaw vehicles on the road and in the fields, a busy shop doing a steady business. Why should he let a strange little man derail his ideas and spook him out of buying a property?

The property was indeed for sale, and two weeks later, Alex was the owner of what would become McKenzie's Mechanical on River Street and Second Avenue Northwest. As the former owner handed Alex the keys, Arne Thorson showed up unbidden with his horse and cart and, without preamble or permission, climbed up onto the roof of the garage and installed a copper lightning rod.

Chapter 7

Verlane Dupray could hold her tongue no longer. Summanus, the god of nocturnal thunder, would never put up with such treatment, and neither would she. It was 1926, and she was an independent woman, not some weakling willing to put up with such treatment for the sake of decorum.

"It is nothing short of slander," she told Janet McKenzie one morning. "You would not credit the things those women are saying about me."

'Those women' were the Moose Jaw Quilting Circle. Some years ago, Janet and Verlane were founding members of the group of a half dozen women who got together every few months to make quilts for the less fortunate. This week they were meeting at the home of Agnes Randolph, who greeted Verlane and Janet at the door.

"It is my solemn duty to tell you that you two are no longer members of the Moose Jaw Quilting Circle," Agnes said and started to close the door in their faces.

"Just a minute, Agnes," Verlane said, putting her sturdy kid leather boot between the door and the jamb. "We helped to start this group. Would you mind explaining yourself?"

"Kindly remove your foot from my door," Agnes said sharply.

"Is there a problem?" asked Margarethe La Salle, a head taller than Agnes and standing right behind her, looming over her shoulder.

"No problem at all," said Verlane, removing her foot from the door. "It is abundantly apparent we have come to the wrong house."

"Clearly," huffed Agnes. "When were you going to tell us that you were run out of Baton Rouge for your shenanigans?"

"My apologies," Verlane said. "You only had to ask. But it's entirely my mistake in thinking that I was associating with women of high quality, when in fact, I was in the midst of a bunch of common gossips." With that, she and Janet turned and walked back to Verlane's Model A Ford.

"I apologize for having you tarred with the brush meant only for me," Verlane said to Janet as they set off. "I thought that intelligent people would take care to inform themselves before making rash assumptions."

"What was that all about?" Janet asked. "And what was that remark about Baton Rouge?"

"It's a tawdry saga, my dear, but I will give you the gist of it. When Arthur and I were first married, we lived in Baton Rouge, where Arthur practiced law. He defended a Negro who was accused of raping a white woman, and when the trumped-up charges were dismissed and the man was set free, people wanted to lynch the poor Negro. They were unsuccessful, I'm happy to say, but they turned on Arthur and called him... well, I won't repeat the words."

"Just for defending a man?"

"For defending a black man, Janet. You see, the Ku Klux Klan had control of the mayor's office in Baton Rouge and held sway over the District Attorney who, I do believe, was a member of one of their dens or whatever they call them. They drummed Arthur out of the Law Society and made it impossible for him to practice in the state of Louisiana."

"But can they do that? I thought America was the home of the free or something."

"They can, and they did. We fought them for a while, but it was just too much. Alice had no end of trouble at school. Our legal fees were higher than Arthur's income, and in the end, we decided to come to Canada, where the Klan has no power. At least, I think that's the case, although I am given to understand they are setting up chapters right here in our fair province."

"Yes, you're right. I saw an advertisement bold as brass in the paper last week offering membership to any white men who might apply. But Verlane, why is Agnes so poorly informed about your situation? Did you not tell her what you just told me?"

"I tried, but Agnes took a dislike to me the second she laid eyes on me, and, I have to confess to my shame, the feeling was quite mutual. So, she began spreading malicious gossip about me, calling me 'that American witch.' It all came to a head a few weeks ago."

"How have I missed all this?" Janet asked.

"I have tried to spare you the tedious drama of it all. But do you recall the tragedy at the Kuzik farm two weeks ago?" Verlane asked. The Kuziks farmed near Pasqua, about eight miles east of Moose Jaw, after buying the farm from another couple from Ukraine who had died in a runaway buggy accident. Janet had heard that there had been a recent death on the Kuzik farm but knew little more than that.

"Well, Agnes and her cronies blame me for the death of Peter and his son Jacob," Verlane said with a sigh. "That's the nub of it right there."

"I hadn't heard that his son died too. How very sad. People who farm that land seem to have the worst luck. But what could you possibly have to do with their deaths?"

"They say I predicted their deaths at a Quilting Circle meeting a few months ago."

"I vaguely recall you saying something about a dream of fire or some such..."

"I spoke of a dream in which I saw a fiery man and boy," Verlane said. "In my dream, they were the firstborn and so they were more susceptible to the curse of lightning. And two weeks ago, lightning came down the Kuzik's stovepipe, through the stove itself, and across the kitchen floor, killing Peter as well as Jacob, who was sitting on his lap. Both were firstborns."

"How could anyone possibly blame you for having a dream?" Janet asked. She understood prairie people to be pragmatists. The climate was extreme and required common sense, practical skills, and good planning to survive. There was little room for superstitious beliefs, but that didn't stop some people from harbouring ill-formed prejudices.

"They say I somehow invoked the lightning, conspired to make it strike the Kuziks to prove my prediction," Verlane said. "In town the other day, Agnes crossed the street to avoid me. She was with two other women from the quilting circle, and I am sure one of them uttered the word 'witch.'"

"It appears as though Agnes Randolph hides behind the skirts of other women," said Janet dismissively as they rattled down the road. "We don't need those women anyway. Their chatter is all about people instead of ideas, which is why I prefer your company. I still have my quilting frame. The two of us started the quilting circle, what has it been, six years ago now? And we did quite well on our own at the beginning, did we not?"

"We did indeed, my girl, we did indeed!" Verlane said. "And anyone who takes Agnes Randolph's side against me can join her in hell."

That almost sounded like another curse, but Janet thought better about making any comment. She was still a bit overwhelmed by Verlane's forthright manner but had grown to like, even to admire, the woman for her outspoken views. She had known Verlane for more than a decade and heard her express many opinions that others at first decried but then adopted months or even years later. Perhaps that was part of Verlane's ability to 'see' into the future, to divine the way events will proceed. She simply had more sense than most and could see how events might play out.

Verlane wheeled the Ford into the McKenzie's driveway and pulled up in front of the house in a cloud of dust. As Janet got out, Verlane reached across the seat and touched her arm.

"I don't mean to pry but... well, has Robert given any more thought to getting a lightning rod?" Arne Thorson was making the rounds and had sold a good many lightning rods in Moose Jaw over the years.

None of the houses equipped with one had ever been struck by lightning, so it was assumed the lightning rods were doing their job.

"He won't have one, Verlane," Janet said. "Much as I do try to encourage him to purchase one, the man is adamant. Says it will only attract lightning to our house."

"Well, lightning was attracted to the Kuziks' house, and tragically, they had no lightning rod," Verlane said. "Lightning's a fact of life out here, my dear. Not like where I come from. In Louisiana, the swamp gas is more likely to kill you than lightning." She chuckled and lit a cigarette.

"I know, Verlane, but... well, I may as well tell you. Robert was only ten when he saw his father killed by lightning in Scotland. Ever since then, he's been terrified of thunderstorms and fears a lightning rod will just introduce death and the devil into our home."

"The poor boy! What an awful thing to see. But Robert should know that the rod takes the lightning's electrical charge and disperses it so it can't come down your stovepipe. I fear what happened to the Kuziks could happen to you and your family without a lightning rod. And that's not a prediction or a curse, by the way. It's just science."

"I understand, and I thank you for your concern, Verlane, but there's nothing for it. Robert wasn't even swayed by the article in *Prairie Farm and Home* last month quoting Mr. Albert Einstein himself praising the lightning rod or the fact that Bejamin Franklin swore by them. It's a lost cause."

Chapter 8

A sharp rap on the front door startled Verlane Dupray out of a waking dream in which she was making her way carefully through a maze of swords stuck in the ground all around her while a small dog yapped silently at her feet. She roused herself from the subconscious mists of her afternoon nap and got up to see who was banging on the front door.

"Mrs. Arthur Dupray?" An RCMP constable stood on the porch while another waited on the front walk. The Dominion Police had joined forces with the Royal Northwest Mounted Police to become the Royal Canadian Mounted Police several years ago, but Verlane still thought of them as forest rangers in their boots, jodhpurs, Sam Browne belts, and Stetsons. And now they were on her doorstep.

"I am *Verlane* Dupray. And you are...?"

"Constable J.V. Deslauriers, madam, of the Royal Canadian Mounted Police. This is Constable R.S. Lund. May we come in?" The young man had a wispy moustache and stood ramrod straight.

"What is this about?"

"If we could talk inside…" The constable took a step forward as the other constable climbed the steps and stood on the porch.

Not wanting to seem rude, Verlane opened the door and let the two police officers come in. She showed them into the drawing room, and once they were all seated, she asked again, "What is this about?"

"Madam, do you know the late Peter Kuzik?"

"I knew *of* him. I never met the man."

"Did you or did you not on the afternoon of April 3rd in this year of our Lord 1926 predict the death of Peter Kuzik and his son Jacob Kuzik?"

"I did not." Verlane did not appreciate being interrogated in her own home. She knew at once the source of the accusations and would not be led into some sort of confession or admission of any kind based on tittle-tattle from Agnes Randolph and her acolytes.

"We have sworn testimony that in fact you not only predicted these two deaths but described the manner in which the victims would die."

"Was there a question in there?"

"Madam did you predict that Jacob Kuzik would die of electrocution?" Const. Deslauriers leaned forward and fixed her with a stare meant to induce fear.

Verlane was having none of it. "I will not answer any more of your questions until I have consulted with legal counsel," she said, standing up. "Unless I am under arrest, I would ask you to leave my home now." The two officers stood and Const. Deslauriers moved a little closer to Verlane.

"Mrs. Arthur Dupray, I hereby arrest you on a charge of conspiracy to commit murder and a further charge of conspiracy to conceal from the authorities your complicity in the death of Peter Kuzik and the death of Jacob Kuzik." Const. Deslauriers showed her a warrant that purported to make that claim.

"Conspiracy?" Verlane looked from one officer to the other in disbelief. "With whom have I conspired? Murder? Am I to be libeled in my own home by idle gossip? And by the way, my given name is Verlane, not Arthur. Even I know that you have to have the correct name if you are going to arrest someone. You cannot arrest Mrs. Arthur Dupray because that person does not exist, so your warrant has no legal effect. It's been more than a decade since women got the vote, you know, and we're allowed to use our own names."

"Lanie? Who's here?" The front door closed, and Arthur Dupray came into the drawing room with their daughter Alice.

"Mr. Arthur Dupray?" inquired Const. Deslauriers.

"I am Arthur Dupray, and this is our daughter, Alice Dupray." They stood on either side of Verlane. "Who the hell are you two boy scouts, and what are you doing in my drawing room?"

"Sir, I am... we have come to arrest your wife..."

"Arrest my wife?" Arthur interrupted. He was tall and commanding, and the two RCMP officers winced as he questioned them. "Are you quite in possession of your faculties, sir? Whatever for?"

Const. Deslauriers proffered the warrant, which Arthur scanned quickly and handed back with a sniff. Alice stood beside her mother. Their auburn hair, intelligent brown eyes, and confident way of carrying themselves left little doubt they were related.

"Sir, I think you'll see all is in order to effect..."

"I see nothing, young man," Arthur said, "except an attempt to arrest an innocent person in their private home on a trumped-up charge no doubt spawned by a town gossip. I would thank you to leave my property, and we will see you in town with legal counsel to answer these ridiculous allegations."

"But sir, I have been sent..."

"The RCMP was only formed twenty minutes ago, son. You'd best tread lightly in my home if you expect your authority to last another twenty minutes." As far as Arthur was concerned, Chief Walter Johnson's Moose Jaw Police took care of the city, and people in the country took care of themselves. These pups looked too young to play any sort of law enforcement role in either area.

"Sir, I must protest," said Const. Deslauriers, taking a step back. "We are only here to do our duty."

"Duty?" asked Alice. "Duty? Is it your 'duty' to accost people in their own home based on hearsay from gossips? Is that what you are saying?"

"But we have a warrant...." Const. Deslauriers said, waving the document feebly. In the constable's limited experience, men challenged the law but never women, who respected the uniform and the legal structure behind it. Or so he believed. He carried on. "It's signed by the..."

"I don't care if it's signed by Prime Minister Mackenzie King himself. Anyone with a printing press can turn out dozens of these," Arthur said with a laugh as he snatched the warrant from the officer's hand. "I am a lawyer and know the Criminal Code as well as anyone and certainly better than you. We know where your detachment is, and we will be there in due course to answer these charges. We are unlikely to flee the country as we have animals to care for. Good day, gentlemen."

The two constables did not move for several awkward moments, nor did the three members of the Dupray family. The frozen tableau seemed destined to be carved in stone until Const. Lund sneezed, the tension broke, and time could move forward.

"We should go..." Const. Lund said quietly, edging toward the door.

Arthur tucked the warrant into his jacket pocket and stepped aside so that Const. Deslauriers could follow his partner. "You have done your duty, officer. We will be in touch. Good day." The two Mounties retreated to the front hall and closed the door quietly behind them on the way out.

"You needn't have come riding in on your white stallion to rescue me, dear," Verlane said when the officers had gone. "The situation was well in hand."

"That's as may be," Arthur said. "But some men still need to be told their place by other men. They won't hear it from a woman."

"I've done nothing to be rebuked for and refuse to countenance such slander."

"Still, you should talk to a lawyer before venturing into their orbit," Arthur said. "Of course, I can't represent you, but I could suggest a few names..."

"What about Scotty McKenzie, Mom?" Alice said. "He's a young guy, pretty sharp, and he'd love to take on a case like this."

"He's fresh out of law school," Arthur said. "We need a man with experience and standing in the community, someone like J.H. Clinton and Sons. Now there's a firm that's been around for a while."

"They do conveyancing and escrow claims, Dad, as you well know. They've never been in a criminal courtroom."

"Well, then why not..." Arthur was about to recommend another of his cronies downtown when Verlane interrupted him.

"Never mind. This business is nothing more than idle chit-chat used by a few catty women trying to tarnish my reputation in this community. I think Mr. McKenzie would be ideal. He's young, brash, and keen as mustard. Contact him, please, Alice dear, and we can put this all behind us."

Chapter 9

Scott McKenzie extended a hand to John Gordon Ross, then pulled out a chair for him to sit on. He'd met the man a few times but was surprised by a telephone call that morning asking if the MP could 'stop by for a chat.' An hour later, he arrived at Scott's law office.

"I'm flattered that you've come to see me, Mr. Ross, but if it's legal advice you're after, I'm sure there are far better attorneys in Moose Jaw and certainly in Ottawa..."

"As an MP, I've got all the lawyers I need, thanks," Ross said and chuckled. "Too many to count, in fact. No, I came to see you on the advice of your father. And I apologize for just dropping in, but it's less formal this way. The reason for my visit is that there are some people, your father among them, who think you might be a good candidate for Moose Jaw City Council."

"My father?"

"And others. Robert wanted to broach the subject with you himself but thought that the suggestion might carry... uh... more weight if it came from my office." Ross thought that Scott would make a good MP one day, and municipal politics was a good proving ground.

"I don't know anything about politics, sir," Scott said. "I scarcely have time to follow the news in the *Times Herald*, although I have read some reports on your work and commend your efforts to encourage farmers to cut back on the plowing. Low till is certainly easier on the land."

"Thank you for your kind words, Scott. And please call me John. Yes, some more progressive farmers are taking it up, but I fear we've already lost a good deal of Saskatchewan topsoil."

"My father and brother, Michael, are quite pleased with the results," Scott said. "I don't know too much about farming, but my dad sure does. And as mentioned, I know even less about politics than I do about farming. I'm still 'wet behind the ears' as Dad might say."

"That's not necessarily a drawback, Scott. Too many people who get into politics love the cut and thrust of it and forget why they're there — to represent and serve their constituents. All of them. It's because you don't want the job that you're an ideal choice, if that makes any sense."

Scott was no stranger to political discourse at the dinner table and around the house while he was growing up. Topics including the cooperative movement, centralized grain trading, and the never-ending debate about the Crowsnest Pass rate for shipping grain were all served up along with the roast beef and mashed potatoes at supper time. Scott hated the mind-numbing minutiae of some of the discussions and tried to steer clear of politics altogether to concentrate on his law practice. Nothing he'd seen since then had changed his mind.

"Sir, I appreciate your confidence in me, but I don't know if I can spare the time away from my law practice just now." Not to mention the possibility of losing clients because of his political views, which up until now he had been careful to keep to himself.

"It's one four-hour meeting a month and maybe a bit of committee work here and there," Ross said. "And there is a small honourarium to compensate you for your time."

"It's not the money, sir, it's..."

"...what clients may think of your political views. Sorry to finish your thought, but it's what almost kept me from getting involved all those years ago. But while you may lose support in some quarters, you gain it in others, so it all comes out in the wash. It's surprising how much you can get accomplished if you don't get too attached to the results."

That last statement stuck in Scott's brain, and the questions it raised wouldn't let him sleep that night. His law practice was picking up, so why was he even thinking about running for office? He had no hobby horses to ride, no pet issues to put forward and champion. It was difficult being in the public eye, so easy to say the wrong thing or ignore the wrong person. On the other hand, he knew about a few of the city administration's problem areas from talking with clients, and there were no doubt other problems that weren't so apparent to the casual eye. He was a single man with no family commitments, so maybe it was his time to serve. But just in case, he talked it over with his father and for once was able to take the offensive with him.

"You've put me in a bit of a spot, Dad, because I don't want to offend your friend Mr. Ross by saying no," Scott said as they sat on the verandah. "But if I say yes and lose, it'll stick to you as well as me."

"Very thoughtful, son. There are no guarantees in politics, not that I give much of a damn what people think about me. You get to be a certain age, and you find you don't care what 'they' might say. But I only suggested to John that he talk to you about the idea, not that you would necessarily accept his invitation."

"I don't know... if this is political favouritism or nepotism or something..." Scott said with a wry chuckle.

"Nothing like that, I assure you. He asked after you, and I suggested you might give the idea some consideration. Politics can be a nasty business, but it is possible to do some good. But it's entirely up to you."

"The thing is, Dad, I think I might take him up on the offer," Scott said with a grin. "If I can count on your support, that is. Don't want to blot the family copybook by losing."

"Congratulations, Scotty," Robert said. "That's the right choice. Win or lose, I'll back you all the way."

Scott McKenzie was elected that spring by a comfortable margin and took his place among the six other men and the Mayor around the council table. He found that there was more than a bit of committee work. And he discovered that most of the councillors did not share his views on the welfare of the indigent or the need to change the cozy way city contracts were awarded.

"We've always done it this way," Councillor Talbot told him. "It seems to work just fine."

"But you don't... that is, *we* don't get competitive bids. We just go with the same contractor or supplier time after time."

"It's a bad system, I agree," Talbot said. "But in my experience, all the other systems are worse. So, we go with the guys we know."

Battling such fiscal laziness was like boxing with fog, so Scott picked his fights and learned how to back another councillor's idea in exchange for mutual support. And, despite his fears, McKenzie Law flourished, in part because of his role and the name recognition that comes with being a city councillor.

"Of course, I'll take the case," Scott said without hesitation when Alice Dupray visited his office. The McKenzies had been friends with the Dupray family for more than a decade.

"Isn't it bad for your law business to defend the Wascana Witch?"

"Don't worry about that. Although your mother will be under a lot of pressure if this goes to trial. Is Verlane up to that sort of scrutiny?"

"She's tough, Scotty. These folks have no idea of the woman they've unleashed with these charges. She's gonna eat them for lunch."

Chapter 10

WASCANA WITCH SENSATION!

~ TRIAL BEGINS TODAY ~

Moose Jaw – Mon Aug 8/27 – The woman dubbed The Wascana Witch goes on trial for her life today. Mrs. Arthur Dupray, 46, is charged with murder in the deaths of Peter Kuzik, 37, and his infant son, Jacob. The Crown claims that Mrs. Dupray called down the bolt of lightning that killed poor Mr. Kuzik and his young son, who was sitting on his father's lap. The police say the defendant predicted the deaths some two weeks before the event and further...

People lined up before dawn to get one of the few dozen public seats inside the courtroom. Latecomers had to be content to linger on the stone courthouse steps and the surrounding lawn in the summer heat and make do with tidbits of second-hand information relayed to them from the trial. Hawkers of every description patrolled the crowd, selling booklets, nostrums, hot dogs, and popcorn. One woman did quite well unloading bits of genuine lightning-blasted rock. A small, dark man leading a cart and horse sold lightning rods as he made his way through what looked like an impromptu carnival. As he walked, the man repeated a short verse in a quiet but insistent tone.

"Spare the rod and share the blame. Watch the world go up in flames. Your protection or your shame. Take the rod and fire's tamed."

Inside the airless courtroom, reporters from the *New York Times* and *The Guardian* stood at the back of the courtroom to write their stories, along with scribes from the *Regina Leader-Post* and the *Moose Jaw Times Herald*. There were three junior lawyers at the prosecution table, along with Crown Counsel James F. Wigmore, KC, who was going over notes for his opening remarks. Scott McKenzie sat with Verlane Dupray at the defendant's table, wondering what he'd got himself into. On the bench, Judge Howard M. Calvert called for order in the court.

"Let me be clear," Judge Calvert said in a resonant baritone borrowed from God. "I will not have my courtroom disrupted in any way during these proceedings. Do not speak unless you are asked a question. Do not talk amongst yourselves or in any way comment on these proceedings, either here or outside my courtroom. If I have made myself clear, Mr. Wigmore, you may begin to prosecute your case."

"Thank you, your Honour. Members of the jury and fellow citizens, this case is built around the word *intent*. That the defendant," Wigmore turned and glared at Verlane Dupray, "did willfully and with malice aforethought conspire to cause the death of Peter Kuzik and his infant son, Jacob."

"Objection, your Honour," Scott McKenzie said, standing beside the defense table. "My learned friend has made a statement, not asked a question."

"Overruled Mr. McKechnie."

"It's McKenzie, your Honour, with respect."

"Overruled. Proceed Mr. Wigmore."

"Thank you, your Honour. The Crown contends that Verlane Dupray did, with malice aforethought, conspire to cause the deaths of Peter and Jacob Kuzik. And we will prove our contention beyond a shadow of a doubt." Wigmore went on at length, citing precedents chapter and verse until the jury was nodding either in agreement or because they were falling asleep. "And, the defendant predicted not only of the deaths of these two unfortunate souls, but the manner of their deaths, *ipso facto* you have no recourse gentlemen of the jury but to return a verdict of 'Guilty' on all charges." Wigmore struck a pose like a triumphant general, basking in adulation for having already won the war.

"Thank you, Mr. Wigmore," Judge Calvert said. "We'll break for lunch and return in sixty minutes."

The judge retired to his chambers and the jury to their jury room. But nobody else went anywhere. People who had lined up for seats were not about to relinquish them to have lunch. There was almost a party atmosphere as they unpacked their sandwiches and thermoses full of soup or tea. They were still stowing away the remains of their snacks when the bailiff entered the courtroom.

"All rise," he said.

People stood laconically and brushed sandwich crumbs from their laps. The judge entered, looked around at the detritus from the picnic, and frowned. "Be seated," he said grumpily. "Please call the jury in from the jury room." The bailiff did so, and the twelve good and true men trooped in slowly and took their seats in the jury box. Inexperienced as he was in trial law, Scott knew he was in trouble. Grumpy judges were never a good thing, and sleepy post-prandial jurors might not be as sharp as they could be.

Still, needs must. He'd just have to step up his game a notch. Or two.

"I'll be brief," he said, rising after lunch to present the case for the defense. "It is physically and scientifically impossible for a person to marshal the forces of lightning in order to cause or even to conspire to cause the death of another person or persons. Unless my learned colleague, Mr. Wigmore can prove beyond a shadow of a doubt that the forces of lightning can in fact be harnessed by one person, and unless he can find someone to actually demonstrate that particular skill to this courtroom, you have no other recourse, gentlemen of the jury, than to return a verdict of 'Not Guilty' on these baseless charges."

Wigmore began his prosecution by putting Agnes Randolph on the stand.

"Just one question Mrs. Randolph – did you on Friday the third day of April in this, the Year of Our Lord 1926, witness Mrs. Arthur Dupray predict the death by lightning of Peter and Jacob Kuzik?"

"I did."

"Thank you, Mrs. Randolph," Wigmore said. "Nothing further, your Honour."

"Mr. McKechnie? Any questions for this witness?" asked Judge Calvert.

"Thank you, your Honour. Good afternoon, Mrs. Randolph. My name is Scott *McKenzie*, and I am the counsel for your friend Verlane Dupray, the defendant in these proceedings, who is sitting there at the table on your left. Like my learned friend, Mr. Wigmore, I have only one question for you, Mrs. Randolph – do you truthfully believe that one person can be so powerful as to harness a force so elemental as lightning?"

Agnes Randolph looked at the Crown Counsel's table for guidance, but Wigmore was stone-faced. She looked at her well-manicured nails and then at the judge. "I don't understand the question, your Honour."

"Repeat the question, Mr. McKechnie. Keep it simple this time."

"Thank you, your Honour. Mrs. Randolph, I'll make this simple, as Judge Calvert has requested. Do you believe that the defendant and your former friend, Verlane Dupray, can control lightning? Answer 'Yes' if you believe she can and 'No' if you believe she can not."

Murmurs rippled through the spectators despite a stern look from Judge Calvert. Verlane smiled slightly. Agnes straightened her back and spoke in a clear voice.

"I believe she predicted those deaths because she has some kind of special powers that we don't know about," she said, looking at Verlane. "And I believe Mr. Kuzik and his son are dead because of it."

"Was that a 'yes' or a 'no' Mrs. Randolph?"

"Yes. It was a 'yes.'"

"And if I may be permitted one more question. On what are those beliefs based?"

"Why, why... I just believe, that's all. Some things you just know, young man. Like belief in the Lord." Agnes Randolph crossed her arms and glared at the counsel for the defense as if he had cursed in church.

"Thank you, Mrs. Randolph. Nothing further, your Honour." Scott sat down and made some notes on his yellow legal pad.

"The Crown now calls noted fulminologist, Fergus Frembd," Wigmore said. A gray, little man was brought in from the antechamber and sworn in. As Frembd settled into the witness box, Wigmore consulted some notes at his table, then rose, looked about the room for a moment as if thinking deep thoughts, and approached the witness stand.

"Mr. Frembd, a person can direct the forces of lightning, wouldn't you agree?"

"Objection, your Honour. Leading the witness." Scott stayed on his feet.

"Sustained. Jury will disregard that last question. Mr. Wigmore, confine your questioning of this witness to questions, not statements."

"Thank you, your Honour," Wigmore said, knowing the seed had been planted in the jurors' minds that a leading expert on lightning might think a person could control it. Now, to help that seed grow.

"Mr. Frembd... let's start at the beginning. What is a fulminologist?"

"A fulminologist," Frembd said slowly, as if talking to a very young child, "is a person who studies lightning."

"And how long have you been a fulminologist?" Wigmore asked.

Wigmore took two full days to present his case and an hour to sum up. The defense took ten minutes.

"In this courtroom, over the past two days, you have heard gossip about paranormal powers," Scott McKenzie began. "You've heard the prosecution's supposition that any one of you could be tossing around lightning bolts like Zeus." Laughter rippled through the audience until Judge Calvert gave them the hairy eyeball, and the place became as quiet as a cloister. "What you haven't heard is any shred of hard evidence to back up the Crown's fanciful charges that a person – any person, much less my client Verlane Dupray – can direct a bolt of lightning. You have heard hearsay, supposition, and plain old gossip. Testimony has been that Mrs. Dupray had a dream. In no way, shape, or form were the Kuzik's names mentioned when Mrs. Dupray related her dream to the ladies of the Moose Jaw Quilting Circle. Nor did she specify that her dream was about lightning. In fact, she testified that she saw in her dream, and I quote: "...a fiery man and boy..." end quote. It was a dream, gentlemen of the jury, not a prediction, and certainly not material to the unfortunate deaths of Mr. Kuzik and his son. It is outrageous that this scurrilous gossip has been brought into this courtroom masquerading as sworn testimony, and so, I submit that you have no other choice but to render a verdict of not guilty of all charges."

Judge Calvert gave the jurors their instructions and encouraged them to come back to him at any time during their deliberations with any questions they may have. Twenty minutes after the jury was sequestered, the foreman knocked on Calvert's chambers door. The judge had barely tucked into his roast beef sandwich.

"Your Honour, sorry to interrupt your lunch, but is twenty minutes too short a time to deliberate?"

"It depends. Have you reached a unanimous verdict?"

"Yes sir, we have, your Honour."

"Then apparently twenty minutes is sufficient time to do so. We will return to the courtroom in fifteen minutes. Justice delayed is justice denied."

James Wigmore hadn't left the courtroom. Nor had Verlane and Scott, who sensed it was going to be a quick verdict either way. Not this quick, though. Wigmore had gone off for a long lunch and a runner had to be sent to fetch him, so the Crown prosecutor entered the courtroom just as Judge Calvert took his seat on the bench.

"Be seated," the judge told the courtroom and everyone sat quietly like obedient pets. "Mr. Foreman, has the jury reached a verdict?"

"We have your Honour," said the Foreman, standing. Verlane gave a quick start, thinking she could be taken off to jail this very afternoon, locked in a cell and kept there for months or perhaps even years, not seeing Arthur, Alice, or anyone else. Perhaps even executed. She shivered, and there was a buzzing in her ears so she could barely hear what the foreman was saying. "We find the defendant, Verlane Dupray, not guilty on all charges." Gasps and murmurs rippled through the crowd until Judge Calvert's thundering voice silenced them.

"I will clear the court if this continues. Mr. Foreman, that is your verdict, and so say you all?" asked the judge.

"We do, your Honour."

"Thank you for your service, gentlemen of the jury," Judge Calvert said. "You are dismissed. The defendant is free to go. Mr. Wigmore... my chambers if you please."

Chapter 11

The rattle of windblown sand against the windows sounded like skeletal hands rolling dice. A dry spell in 1929 had turned into a drought in 1930 and a dustbowl since then. So little rain had fallen that some young children had never seen it. The summer of 1935 was particularly dry, and the wind sent a goodly portion of Robert McKenzie's topsoil east to Manitoba.

Like an unwanted guest, summer hung around too long, making Robert edgy and robbing him of sleep. As Janet softly snored beside him, he thought about the Belgians and the loss of Caesar all those years ago. Cleo was gone now, too, and Duke as well, but they were given gentle deaths as befits gentle animals. Not like Caesar, stabbed by lightning in his own pasture. It was as if the fates had conspired against Robert, perhaps for his hubris in thinking he could breed Belgians in such a harsh climate, although Cleo and Duke had thrived. So, was Caesar's death further proof of the McKenzie Curse?

Thinking about the Belgians got Robert thinking about his breeding program. He was raising quarter horses now because they were versatile and easy to ride. That got him thinking that maybe it was time to relax a little and enjoy what he and Janet had worked so hard for over the past quarter century. They should go into town for dinner some night soon, even take in a movie. *Napoleon* was playing at the Capitol, which seemed appropriate somehow, given the empire building that was going on in Europe. The Italians were spoiling for war, and the Germans were almost doubling the size of their naval fleet while burning books and rounding up Jews. It was a terrible time to be alive.

Robert must have slept because he woke up as the day was breaking, although he was more tired than when he went to bed. As he got dressed, he vowed to get more exercise so that he would sleep better. Maybe he'd ride out this morning and check on the herd and their summer range. It was still early, but there was already heat in the air as he opened the barn door and relished the rich aroma of horses, hay, and harness. The sun angled in through the hayloft window, and motes of heifer dust and dander floated in the honey-coloured air. It was his favourite time of day. There was no pressure, no ringing telephones, or decisions to be made. The calm before the storm.

"Hey now, Peg," he said to the chestnut quarter horse who snuffled and nickered a greeting. "Would you like some sweet hay?

And how about some oats?" He called the stallion Pegasus in homage to Zeus, figuring the god of thunder wouldn't attack the horse who carried his lightning bolts or the man who rode him.

Demand for horses had dropped off when the automobile came into vogue during the twenties. Almost everyone had a car and insisted on driving it around at top speed, frightening the children and livestock. But six years into the Depression, gas and money were scarce, and horses were once again in high demand. Even old nags could be put into a harness to tow Bennett Buggies – horse-drawn automobiles with the engine removed and the reins going through the open windshield – named after Prime Minister R.B. Bennett.

There seemed to be no end to the hard times. Jobs were scarce, people were hungry, and crops were poor, yet wheat wasn't selling for much more than it did before the crash. Unlike most, Robert had enjoyed steady contracts with Robin Hood almost since the company started milling wheat in Moose Jaw back in 1909. His crops were more productive because he used dryland farming techniques such as low till and stubble retention. Still, without any moisture at all, the soil was as fine and dusty as sifted flour. The sound of a motor car pulling into the farmyard derailed his train of thought.

"Hey Dad," Michael called as he entered the barn. "Thought I'd find you here. We gonna go look at them cattle this morning?"

"Good to see you, Mike. Yeah. We'll ride out after coffee, while it's still cool, if that's OK with you. How's Jenny and that little girl of yours?"

"Amelia's excited for her eighth birthday next week, and that's something I wanted to talk to you about."

"She's still got her eye on that colt, doesn't she?"

As if on cue, the three-year-old whinnied and snorted as he moved back and forth in his stall. Like most youngsters, he was eager to be out and about.

"You bet she does. Even has a name picked out. Blaze." The colt was a deep chestnut like her sire Pegasus with a startling bolt of white right above her eyes.

"Well, I figured as much, so I asked an old friend of mine to work with her a little bit. What Duncan McCain doesn't know about horses isn't worth knowing. So, Blaze is nicely gentled now and not easily startled," Robert said. "Amy will have no trouble getting used to him."

"Thanks, Dad. I've heard Duncan's good with horses. I picked up a swell little saddle and blanket from Alf Brigham, so next week, we'll put it all together."

"Help me get these animals out into the pasture, and then we'll go inside and have a cup of coffee. We can leave Pegasus and Bella in their stalls and saddle them up after breakfast to go have a look at the cattle, OK?" Most of Robert's beef herd was on summer range just south of town.

"Sounds good, Dad," Michael said.

The two men led the horses individually out onto the pasture to stretch their legs. The colt, in particular, gamboled and capered about like a new lamb. There wasn't much forage, but the animals had already been given hay and oats, so they were content to loaf around the pasture, with some of them already seeking shade under the cottonwoods along the fence line, even though it was barely eight am.

Of his three sons, Robert thought Michael looked most like him. They both had copper-coloured hair, bushy brows, deep-set eyes on either side of a sharp nose, and the lopsided grin of shy men who often laugh in spite of themselves. Both of them would rather be among animals than their own kind, so they were comfortable in each other's company, spending hours together and barely saying a word. After coffee, they went back out to the barn, saddled Pegasus and Bella, and set out, planning on being back by early afternoon before the day grew unbearably hot.

"Thought any more about taking over the farm?" Robert asked as they crossed Spring Creek. The watercourse was almost dry, and the soil around its banks was cracked and barren. Even the hardy wolf willow was drooping and brown.

"Any time you want me to," Michael said. "But what'll you do with yourself if you're not farming? Can't see you joining the geezers on coffee row every morning." Robert was only fifty-six and looked a decade younger.

"Oh, I'll keep on breeding horses, I guess. But it'd be good to let go of the day-to-day stuff. Your mother and I might even take a holiday. There's this place called Scotland. You may have heard of it."

"Ha ha. I think someone may have mentioned it a time or two."

"I'd love to take your mother there, back to Nairn to see where I was born."

"She'd love that, Dad," Michael said. "Any time you want to go, we got you covered here at Home Farm. Don't put it off too long."

"Good advice, son. We'll start planning something for maybe next spring. I hear the Scottish weather's particularly nasty in the spring. Meanwhile, I won't be bored here. John's asked me to do a little work for him."

John Gordon Ross was a well-to-do farmer who had been the Liberal MP for Moose Jaw for the past decade. He and Robert were both proponents of dryland farming methods, and Ross wanted McKenzie to spread the word among farmers in the riding. There was some federal money available to encourage no-till farming, although many farmers were still of the mind that you had to turn the soil, that farmland was only productive if you put it under the plow. We've always done it this way, they'd say, even as they lost half their topsoil to the wind.

"Well, you know I'm doing my best to spread the dryland gospel," Michael said. "The soil in that one-quarter section that I left in stubble last fall has a lot more tilth than our other fields. And it held the snow and moisture longer than the rest this spring. Meant that seeding was a bit late, but it's a fair trade off."

"That's my boy," Robert said proudly. Michael was the only one of his sons to embrace farming. Alexander was doing well with his garage in town and at least had a passing relationship with farming through repairing the machinery. Scott studied to be a lawyer and hung out his shingle in a refurbished house on Langford Crescent downtown. Both Scott and Alex leased their quarter sections to Michael for a nominal fee.

Despite the drought, Robert's cattle herd south of town looked well-fed. The yearlings were almost ready to be trucked to the feedlot for finishing before going to market, and a third of the heifers were in calf, so there would be a good crop of little ones next spring.

The day had begun under a cornflower blue prairie sky, but by late morning a fast-moving system rumbled in from the west, with lowering clouds and a wind that stirred the dust and pushed the tumbleweeds up against the fence line. As Michael and Robert turned the horses for home, fat drops of rain raised puffs of dust on the ground and speckled the horses' hides.

"We ought to get a move on..." Robert said, but the rest of his words were lost to a mighty crack of lightning that spooked both horses. Pegasus reared, threw Robert into a clump of Russian thistle and galloped off across the prairie.

"Dad! Are you OK?" Michael hopped off Bella and ran to where his father was struggling to his feet. There was another crack and a shaft of lightning shimmered between the roiling clouds above them. The two men had to shout to be heard above the wind.

"I'm OK, Mike, thanks," Robert said, getting up and brushing thistle seeds from his sleeves and pantlegs. "My dignity's more bruised than my bones. Thought I was a better horseman than that." He felt like the arrogant Bellerophon bucked off by Pegasus after the horse was bitten by a fly sent by Zeus.

"I can take Bella to get Peg if you want to wait here."

"No, Peg's OK," Robert said. "Let's get Bella out of the line of fire."

It doesn't take much to be the tallest thing on the prairie during a thunderstorm and right now that was Bella, who stood almost fifteen hands at the withers. Michael took her reins and followed his father down into a nearby coulee.

"We'll get down in here and we'll..." Robert went rigid as the lightning passed through him into the ground, and he collapsed at Michael's feet. Bella shied, and Michael let go of her reins and ran to his father. Only then did he hear the crack and feel the electricity in the air.

"Dad! Dad!" Michael shouted above the pummeling wind. Robert was slumped over sideways and absolutely still. Michael tried to pull him into a sitting position, but the life had been blasted out of him. Robert's body was fused and rigid. Wind and tears stung Michael's eyes as he held his father in his arms and watched the storm dance away across the prairie, crackling with fire.

<u>Part Two 1936 - 1965</u>

Chapter 12

*When I come to the plains I
come on a train
And the train was the CPR
It took three weeks to get to
Wascana Creek
And that's fast for the CPR.
I got off in the Jaw and
went into a bar
Owned by the CPR
And they watered the beer
so all around me I hear
God damn the CPR!*

Geoffrey Ursell

Danny Siggelow (Siggy to his buddies back in New Brunswick) wasn't sure whether working in the Moose Jaw railyards was worse during the summer or the winter. In January, your mitts stuck to the cold steel, your breath froze in your lungs, and there was the very distinct possibility of dying of hypothermia or at least being hit by a shunted car. Summers were brutal, and the summer of 1938 was particularly bad. You could fry an egg on the drag box, the air was so dry you couldn't get a breath, and there was the distinct possibility of dying of heat exhaustion or being hit by a shunted car. The rest of the year was no screaming hell either, so Siggy arrived at the conclusion that working in the yards at any time of the year was a bad proposition, even if the pay was OK. So, when a conductor called in sick, Siggy jumped at the chance to get out of the yards and ride down to Portal as a substitute conductor on a train of sixty-two empty boxcars and hoppers being taken back across the US border.

The engineer was Abner Hildebrandt, who'd been with the CPR for almost as long as Siggy had been alive. He felt lucky to be riding with Ab and not with some of the other engineers who treated their conductors with contempt at best and sometimes with outright cruelty. Ab was different. He was in love with railroading and thought everyone else should be too, so he helped guys like Siggy to learn not just the job but the craft of being a railroader hauling twenty-five hundred tons of steel across the landscape.

They headed east out of the yards on a hot August afternoon, crossed the Moose Jaw River and rolled through Pasqua. The conductor's main job was to watch for signals, speed limits, and track changes, and holler the information to the engineer. He also had to watch for obstructions on the track. Stalled automobiles. Small children putting pennies on the tracks and straying dangerously close to the train trying to see the result of their efforts. The conductor had to be vigilant all the time. Siggy thought that it was a far more interesting job than working in the yards.

Southeast from Pasqua there were fewer people and not many crossings, so they could get up a head of steam through Wilcox, Milestone, and Yellowgrass, whose enduring claim to fame was recording the hottest day ever in Canada just one year before – Monday, July 5, 1937 – when the temperature climbed to 114 degrees Fahrenheit. The event was quickly commemorated on a bronze sun suspended from a wooden frame beside the highway.

The train picked up speed through Midale, Macoun, and Bien Fait, which the locals pronounced BEEN fate, and headed toward the US border town of Portal, North Dakota, where the engineer and conductor could get a break while the trains were swapped out. Then they'd head north again to Moose Jaw with another train.

Most of the 200-mile trip south was through the late afternoon and on into the night, so Siggy looked at the stars when he had a moment. He could identify the Big Dipper and Orion but mostly they just looked like pinpricks in a big piece of black velvet. His Grade 8 Science teacher told them about the vast distances between the planets and the stars, and he tried to imagine how long a light year was and whether anyone would ever go to outer space as they did in the pulp magazines you could buy at the drugstore for a dime.

The train was just north of Roche Percee when the stars were overwhelmed by gloomy black clouds driven by a belligerent wind out of the Dakotas. Siggy could smell rain in the air even though the day had been as dry as dust. He hollered out to the engineer.

"Hey Ab, do ya think we'll beat this storm to Portal?"

"She's moving fast so mebbe not, but we'll give 'er a good go." Ab eased the throttle out a bit and the train surged as it settled into the slightly higher speed. An increase or decrease of just a few miles an hour changed the way the train reacted to the rails and to itself – how the cars followed each other around a curve or rattled across a cattle guard.

"Quite a bit of lightning up there," Siggy said, looking warily up at the sky. "We gonna be OK?"

"Oh, sure, young fella. Tracks are grounded, don't ya see? Takes the charge off into the ground, so we're OK. Hey, what the...?" Ab narrowed his eyes to stare as far as he could down the darkened tracks. "You got good young eyes. You see the signal for Roche Percee?"

"I don't see anything. It's just black out there." Siggy was starting to get worried. Ab knew every inch of the track, knew within a minute when they'd reach a particular signal or crossing.

"Should be hereabouts somewhere, so we better slow down 'til we see what's what," Ab said, pushing in the throttle almost all the way. "Don't want to hit a moose or maybe a car on the tracks."

Neither man heard the massive crack until after the sky opened up and more than fifty thousand volts of electricity rampaged through the engine they were in, crackled along the half-mile string of cars, and then danced off down the tracks into the night. The rubber mat Siggy stood on was melted to his boots, sending off an acrid smell that competed with the powerful aroma of ozone in the air. The stanchions Siggy held onto were as hot as a stovepipe, so he let go as Ab hauled the train to a stop.

"I can't move my feet," Siggy shouted as a high-pitched pinging filled his ears. "I'm glued to the damn floor."

Ab got a pry bar from under the engineer's seat and stuck it under Siggy's shoes, separating him from the congealing rubber. Ab had been sitting in the engineer's horse-hair-cushioned wooden chair when the lightning struck and was almost unaffected by the bolt. But he didn't waste any time hanging around.

"We gotta get offa this train, kid. C'mon. We may get hit again."

"I'm coming, I'm coming," Siggy said. He stumbled through the engine in his gummy boots and left gluey bits of rubber sole on each tread of the corrugated steel stairs as he descended to the coarse gravel ballast and followed Ab to a coulee a short distance from the tracks.

"You get down," he told Siggy. "Down low on the ground. Lay flat as you can and don't move."

Warm rain washed over them, and both men were soaked to the skin in less than a minute, but Siggy figured being wet was better than being fried. The lightning capered about in the sky above, dancing from cloud to cloud as the thunderclaps got farther apart. Four Mississippi. Five Mississippi. Siggy wanted to move, to get away, but Ab held his shoulder to the ground.

"Stay low. You can't outrun it. They say lightning don't strike in the same place twice, but that just ain't true," he said. "Lightning strikes where it wants to and may hit the same spot a couple, three times. So mebbe, it'll leave us alone and go back to the train 'cause it's bigger."

They crouched even lower as the skies hurled down another yellow and blue bolt that shimmered along the length of the train and continued sizzling down the tracks behind it. The engine and railcars seemed to shiver in place after the lightning passed, like a dog shaking off water. Siggy was shaking too, thinking that he could have been on that train and maybe dead by now if it wasn't for Abner Hildebrandt. The clouds scudded off to the northwest as quickly as they had come, leaving a slice of starry sky and a gibbous moon.

"C'mon, son, let's get a move on. Folks'll be wondering what happened to us," Ab said, getting up and looking around. "Can you walk in those gummy shoes?"

"Yeah, they're almost dry now. Would the train still run?" Siggy asked. "I mean, could we still... ?"

"Wouldn't risk it," Ab said. "Could be hot. It could still be electrified for all we know. All the gauges could be fried. Never had this happen in all my years, and I've seen a lot of lightning. Gotta get the maintenance crew in here, go over her from stem to gudgeon, see what works and what don't."

"You said the tracks are supposed to be grounded, though!" That was definitely the rule around the yards, otherwise the static electricity generated by the cars rolling back and forth, especially in the summer heat, could cause a fire or explosion in one of the tanker cars. Every rookie knew that. That's why each and every car was grounded. Or should be.

"Damn betcha they're s'posed to be grounded," Ab said, shaking his gray head.

"Which is why I think somebody either forgot to do their job or..."

"...or sabotaged the tracks intentionally? Why? For a trainload of empty grain and tanker cars?"

"Likely forgot, then. Can't think of why they'd wanna kill us. Probably more people die from stupidity than intent."

"So now what?"

"Well, it's getting light, so that'd make it about half past five," Ab said, poking his head above the coulee like a gopher and squinting south as if he could see all the way to Portal. "When were we due to arrive?"

"Midnight, maybe just after."

"Five hours is more than a little late. Those Yanks get antsy if their trains don't show up on time, so they may have sent a scouting party up the line," Ab said. "We'll walk down to meet 'em. Walk close to the track but not on it. Even the ballast might still be hot." They climbed out of the coulee and made their way beside the tracks heading southeast toward Portal, four or five miles away and the sun began to warm the day.

Chapter 13

Thunderbolt trainmen spared
Railroad Demands Answers

MOOSE JAW (Wed Aug 17 1938)– Two Moose Jaw men escaped with their lives when lightning struck the train they were driving. Abner Hildebrandt, 46, was the engineer Tuesday night when disaster struck. "We just got out of there in time," he said. His conductor, Danny Siggelow, 30, lost his shoes in the incident but was otherwise unharmed. "I thought we were dead," he said. The railway commended the two men...

Before the commendation came a very private grilling by railroad brass on both sides of the border, asking Ab and Siggy just what the hell happened to their train out there by Roche Percee. Sure, thought Siggy, it was 'their' train now that it had been hit by lightning. The questions continued. Why did they drive into the storm? Were they exceeding the speed limit for that stretch of track and therefore more likely to encounter the worst of the storm? What measures did they take, if any, to ensure the train was properly shut down before exiting the engine? It was tough, but the grilling didn't last long.

When the brass got wind of the public support for 'The Thunderbolt Trainmen' and somebody pointed out the PR value, they changed their tune. Now, Ab and Siggy were 'valued employees to be commended for their valiant actions.' Never mind that they jumped from the train as soon as they could and to hell with shutting anything down. Needs must.

Abner and Siggy were reluctant celebrities when they got back to Moose Jaw. Siggy couldn't pay for a drink anywhere in town. Men called him Thor and Thunderbolt as they clapped him on the back and called for another round. Women sidled up to him and engaged him in conversation, a new experience for him. And his landlord gave him a month's free rent.

The best thing to come out of the whole adventure was that Siggy became a certified conductor. After the grilling and the accusations, the Railway commended him for his 'brave actions during the incident' and promoted him to permanent conductor status with Abner Hildebrandt as his engineer on the run back and forth to Portal. It was a three-days-on, three-days-off shift, and the pay was better than working in the yards. So was the chance of survival, lightning storms notwithstanding.

The press soon dropped the feel-good thunderbolt story when the serious news season began in September. Canada's Prime Minister, Mackenzie King, went to Germany to meet with Chancellor Adolf Hitler and was so impressed with the glory of the Third Riech that he wrote in his diary that Hitler "...truly loves his fellow man and his country." In England, Neville Chamberlain declared 'peace in our time' as the machinery of war geared up across Europe and Asia. Hitler sent troops into the Sudetenland, and Nazi-led mobs destroyed a thousand Jewish shops in Austria on what became known as *Kristallnacht*. National belligerence was in season.

Siggy was glad to be out of the limelight. He settled into the autumn season happy to have a steady job on the railway and a nice place to live that was close to work. Then he got a telephone call.

"Hello, my name is Verlane Dupray, and I'd like to talk with you about your lightning experience this past summer," said in a warm voice dripping with southern honey.

"Why?" was the only thing Siggy could think of to say. He wanted to put the whole thing behind him.

"Young man, you have had a pro*found* experience, surviving a lightning strike like that. I have hesitated in calling you for fear of upsetting your recovery from the incident." She had a courtly way of speaking, and Siggy was almost hypnotized by her lilting rhythm.

"I'm OK," he said. "Still got a bit of ringing in my ears but…"

"I have invited your colleague, Mr. Hildebrandt…"

"Ab?" Siggy asked.

"Abner Hildebrandt, yes. He is your engineer, is he not?"

"He surely is," said Siggy after a pause. He got buffaloed by *Is he or is he not* questions.

"Well, I wonder if you might have time to come to my home tomorrow afternoon and tell me about your experience," she said. "Mr. Hildebrandt will also be here. I could send a car."

"No, I got a car," Siggy said. "And I could give Ab a ride out there if you want." Last year, Siggy bought a 1926 Ford Model T Roadster with the money he had saved from working on the railroad. He didn't drink much and certainly didn't gamble, so he saved up $125 in less than a year, even after sending money back home to New Brunswick every month.

"That would be most kind of you. Shall we say two p.m. tomorrow afternoon?"

The next day, Siggy was getting dressed when he heard someone droning a sing-song verse just outside his window. He parted the curtains to see a small dark man leading a horse and cart up and down the block, repeating a little rhyme.

"Spare the rod and share the blame. Watch the world go up in flames. Your protection or your shame. Take the rod and fire's tamed." On the side of his cart was a sign reading:

A. Thorson Lightning Rods

The man was gone by the time Siggy was dressed and got outside. He looked up at the roof. Did his house need a lightning rod? Was he prone to getting hit? Maybe he should track down Mr. A. Thorson and buy a lightning rod from him. But not today. After breakfast, Siggy got in his car and drove over to Ab's place, where he refrained from tooting the horn because it sounded like the strangled call of a sick duck. Instead, he waited a minute, and sure enough, Ab came out to see who was parked in front of his house.

"Want a ride out to Mrs. Dupray's place?" he asked when Ab opened the door.

"I was gonna swing by your place and ask you the same thing," Ab said. "Ya beat me to it! Give me a minute, and I'll be right out. Just gotta get something." Ab emerged from the house a few minutes later, carrying a Gladstone bag, which clunked as he threw it into the space behind the front seat.

"Thanks for the ride. Nice little flivver you got here," Ab said as he got into the passenger seat. "Treat you alright?"

"No problems at all, considering she's a dozen years old. It's a pretty simple motor, and I can usually fix anything that goes wrong."

He and Ab were both on three days off, and Siggy didn't mind going for a drive in the country, especially with Ab, who always had interesting things to say about the world around them. Siggy followed Verlane's directions, and twenty minutes later, they rolled up in front of a large farmhouse where two women greeted them in the broad driveway.

"Welcome. I am Verlane Dupray," the older woman said as she extended her hand when Siggy got out of the car. "And this is my daughter, Alice."

Harps played. Angels sang. Clouds parted, and sunbeams streamed down from heaven. Siggy was in love. He'd seen Alice in town a few times but didn't know her name and never really noticed until now how absolutely perfect she was in every way. How her smile made him weak, and her eyes looked right at him, which she was doing right now and offering her hand to shake.

Was he supposed to say something? No, she was talking.

"Thanks for coming," Alice said, holding his hand a little longer than seemed necessary but not nearly long enough as far as Siggy was concerned. She could hold his hand all afternoon if she wanted to. "You must have been incredibly clever and brave to get out of that train alive."

By now, everyone had read the account in the newspapers, embellished by talk in barber shops and beauty salons. *The Thunderbolt Trainmen* and all that. Siggy always smiled, ducked his head, and said aw shucks or it was nothing. But with Alice, he felt he could be honest.

"I wasn't clever nor brave," he said. "I was scared stupid. And if it wasn't for Ab here, I'd've still been on that train when the second one hit, and I'd be a cooked goose."

"We got lucky," Ab allowed.

"Let's go inside where we can talk further," Verlane said.

Larch logs gave off a sweet scent as they burned in a baronial fieldstone fireplace in the vast living room. Verlane directed Siggy and Ab to a couple of easy chairs while she and Alice sat across from them on a burgundy brocaded sofa.

Once tea had been served on the low glass table between them, Verlane began, "What did it look like, the lightning that hit your train?"

"Couldn't say, ma'am," Ab said. "Didn't see it. Just hit us. Wham! Like that."

"We were inside the cab, so I didn't really see it so much as feel it," Siggy said.

"Was it a bolt, or a current or... How did it feel? Or sound? Sorry to pepper you with questions, but it's just so fascinating."

"Well, that first one was sudden, that's for sure," said Ab, while Siggy gazed at Alice. "It was like all the air went out of the cab, and I couldn't breathe. Then it went kinda snap, like something had broken, and a second later there was this big crack, like a bullwhip."

"Where were you, Siggy?" Alice was looking right back at him.

He would have to speak. Say something. "My shoes were stuck on the mat." Brilliant. Eloquent.

"What kind of mat?" Alice wanted to know.

He wished she'd keep talking. Her voice had the same southern drawl as her mother, but not as syrupy. In fact, it was perfect. But to keep her talking, he would have to answer the question. "Thick rubber," he said stupidly. "Because sometimes friction builds up static electricity on a train, so you don't want to get a shock and rubber's an insulator."

"And you didn't get a shock?"

"No I guess I didn't."

"Where were you Ab?" Verlane asked. "Were you on a rubber mat, too?"

"No, ma'am, I was up in the engineer's chair, a kind of a stuffed chair that turns on a wooden pedestal like a captain's chair, so I can reach all the controls. Engineer sits up front on the left, and the conductor rides a little further back on the right."

"Are you firstborn?" Verlane asked abruptly.

"What? Me? No ma'am, I got an older brother," Ab said. "Well, I did, but he passed a few years ago."

"Was he ever struck by lightning?"

"No, I don't think so. I guess he'd've told me if he was."

"And you, Danny?"

"Siggy. Everyone calls me Siggy."

"Are you the firstborn in your family, Siggy?"

"Yes, ma'am. I got two sisters younger than me. They're still at home in New Brunswick."

Verlane and Alice exchanged a look.

"So, what happened after you got off the train?" Alice asked Siggy.

"Well, we got down in the coulee, and the train got hit again."

"Did you see it this time?"

"Yes ma'am. The light was almost too bright to see, if you know what I mean, but it was kind of blue with yellow around the edges, and it just sort of crackled all up and down the train," Siggy said. "There wasn't any lightning bolt or anything. It just seemed to be everywhere, like a net."

"Do you think the two lightning strikes were the same?" Verlane asked.

"No idea. Couldn't say 'cuz I couldn't see the first one." Ab scratched his chin. "All I can say is the first one was all of a sudden and the second one kind of... lingered for a moment or two. But does that mean there's two different kinds of lightning we have to watch out for?"

"There are at least half a dozen types of lightning, and you can get two or three types in the same storm," Verlane explained. "There's cloud to cloud, cloud to ground, ball lightning, blue jets, sprites – there's even ground lightning, which can kill you just as fast as anything else. So, lying flat on the ground might not have been the best idea. But there I go again, rattling on like some grade schoolteacher."

Alice watched Siggy as he listened to her mother, watched the way he tilted his head when she spoke, and the way he answered her questions without guile or artifice. He had a sweet face, open and trusting. She felt her own face colour a little and wondered if he'd seen her watching him, but he was still listening to Verlane, absolutely focused on her.

"Any questions, either of you?" Verlane asked.

"Well, I heard it doesn't strike twice in the same place," Siggy said, "but we got hit twice. Not sure if that's a question but..."

"Lightning is attracted to... well, in this case, your train," Verlane said. "That's a big piece of metal out there on the empty land, so it's attractive to lightning. And contrary to what you heard, lightning very often strikes the same place twice. Makes sense, doesn't it, because it's attracted to something on the ground. A tree. A telegraph pole. In this case, your train."

"If you'd like to see a piece of it..." Ab opened the Gladstone bag at his feet and pulled out a blackened piece of smooth metal the size of a dinner plate. "This is a piece of the drag box, which is part of the coupling mechanism on the train. It's tough, hardened steel, and yet, look what that lightning did. Polished it like onyx and carved it up like a Sunday roast."

"May I..." Verlane asked, reaching for the hunk of metal.

"Careful. It's heavy," he said as he handed it to her.

"It's so smooth," Verlane said. "I don't know what I expected, but this is like polished stone or something." She handed it back to Ab.

"Polished by the lightning, I guess," he said as he tucked the piece of metal back into the Gladstone bag. "Railroad prob'ly wouldn't like me takin' it, but I figured I had to have a souvenir."

"Have you ever heard of the McKenzie Curse?" Alice asked. "Either of you?"

"I think I heard somethin' about it," Ab said. "Some fella down on coffee row told me about it a while back. Didn't believe him then, and I don't believe it now. Ennaway, neither of us is a McKenzie."

"It may still be plaguing that family, though," Verlane said. "I can see it unfolding in the next few years."

"Why do you say that?" Ab asked her.

"I can see things that will be, Mr. Hildebrandt. And I can see that the McKenzie family is not done with lightning just yet. It follows people around. Especially firstborns." She looked directly at Siggy.

"But lightning can't follow a person," Ab said. "With respect, Mrs. Dupray, it just can't be true. Don't make sense."

"It is attracted to some more than others," Verlane said. "Perhaps it's because they have a lot of iron in their blood. You know, it is a fact that men are four times as likely as women to be struck by lightning, and it is also a fact that men have more iron in their blood than women. The two facts together are merely a coincidence, but an interesting one, don't you think? But, of course, that's only one of many explanations. Science is still confused about the phenomenon."

The sun was almost down, and the air was cooling off by the time Ab and Siggy left the Dupray farm and drove back into town. Neither man spoke until they pulled up in front of Ab's place.

"Wanna come in for a minute or two?" he asked.

"Sure, if that's OK. I got a few questions I'd like to ask you."

The house was neat and tidy, unlike the homes of most bachelor railroaders. Ab poured them each a glass of beer, and they sat down on a couple of easy chairs in the living room.

"So, what do you want to know, Siggy?"

"Mrs. Dupray talked about seeing things... omens... in her mind. Seeing the future and all that. Well, I didn't want to be rude asking her too much about that, but what do you think, Ab? Is she on the level?"

"I'd say she is. Don't know as how I believe in that sort of thing. But it appears she believes in that sort of thing, so I guess that's good enough for me."

"I don't know much about all that spooky, other-world stuff," Siggy admitted. "Just gives me the creeps."

"Most of it's just myths and folk tales, Siggy. But there's some pretty good stories written about it. You read much?"

"I sure do, Ab, and I gotta say, you sure have a helluva lot of books."

Siggy was admiring the large bookcase along one wall in Ab's living room. There were some titles he recognized from the Moncton library back home, but other books he'd never heard of – *The Seven Pillars of Wisdom, Ulysses, Pygmalion, The Beautiful and the Damned.*

"My wife died some years ago," Ab said, "and I find if I can lose myself in a book for a while, I don't miss her quite as much. She was a great reader as well. We built up this library together over thirty years. You know, if you want a good book on spooky stuff, I got one for you." He chose a book from the shelves and handed it to Siggy. On the dust cover was a painting of a man looking at himself in the mirror.

"*The Picture of Dorian Gray* was written almost half a century ago, but it still puts the wind up me," Ab said.

"What's it about?"

"Well, if I told you, you wouldn't have to read it," Ab said with a chuckle. "Ennaway, it's about a fella who makes a deal with the devil, so he'll stay young forever. That's all I'll say. You could borrow it if you like."

"Thanks, Ab. I'd like that. Boy, you could start a library," Siggy said.

"That's where they'll all wind up when I'm gone. To the library. It's in my will."

"Got any books about love?" The beer was loosening Siggy's tongue.

"I saw the way you were looking at Alice this afternoon. She's a beauty, ain't she?"

"Yeah, but I don't know anything about that sort of stuff. I just get flustered and tongue-tied."

"I also saw the way Alice was looking at you."

"She was?"

"She certainly was. And I think she liked what she saw."

"What's that?"

"You're a decent chap, Siggy. So just keep being a decent chap, and you'll be in with a chance. Don't be someone you ain't."

Siggy drove home that night with a tumble of thoughts rolling through his mind. What if Alice actually liked him? How could he act normal around her when she made him feel anything but normal? It was confusing but also encouraging. Life was funny. If that guy hadn't got sick, and his train hadn't been struck by lightning, then he'd never have met Alice. Siggy went to sleep that night on top of the world.

Chapter 14

The Depression and drought hung on like grim death. Work was scarce, money was tight, and almost three million people were out of work. For years, thousands of unemployed single men lived in relief camps operated by the Canadian government, where they were paid a subsistence wage to clear brush or build military bases, like the one south of Saskatoon. Dundurn could house 2500 unemployed men and rarely had fewer than 1500. By 1938, most of the work camps had run their course and were being phased out, releasing thousands of unemployed men into the wilds of society.

Nick Rizzo was among the men 'discharged' from Dundurn because of 'operational changes.' In other words, now that the cheap grunt labour had done most of the heavy lifting, the military could move in and add all the good stuff. Nick knew there was no work in Saskatoon because that's where he'd been before Dundurn, so he made his way southeast toward Regina, walking a lot and hopping freights when he could along the rail line through Hadley, Kenniston, and Davidson.

A railroad bull in Chamberlain told him there might be some farm work around Moose Jaw, about forty miles due south, so Nick walked down the road to where Highway 11 continued southeast to Regina and Highway 2 branched off due south to Moose Jaw. Highway 2 wasn't much of a highway, and there was little traffic. In several hours, only two vehicles went by – a tractor driven by an old guy who waved to him and a sedan driven by a well-dressed guy who didn't. It was mid-afternoon when a Mack truck loaded with gravel rumbled by. When Nick heard the groan of the brake shoes grinding against the drums, he turned and sprinted down the road to where the truck had rolled to a stop.

"Climb in, son," said the driver, a stout man in his middle years. "Goin' ta Moose Jaw, so I can take ya that far ennaway."

"Thank you, sir, that's exactly where I'm going," Nick said, closing the door as the truck gained speed. There was still a breeze because the doors had no windows, but at least there was a windshield, unlike some of the earlier models of Mack trucks Nick had worked on.

"Name's Wilf," the driver said, extending a meaty paw.

"Nick," said Nick, shaking his hand.

"Come far?"

"Just started out from Chamberlain this morning. Looking for work."

“What kind of work?”

“Well, anything, really. I just did a stint at Dundurn, building the army barracks,” Nick said. “But I used to work as a mechanic on trucks like this one up in Saskatoon. Before... you know...”

“Dundurn, eh? Hear that place is shuttin’ down.”

“Well, not entirely, but a few weeks ago, they kicked out the grunt labour anyway. Told us they didn’t need us anymore.”

“So why Moose Jaw?”

“Railroad cop told me there might be work there, fixing farm machinery, that kind of thing.”

“Yup, might could be at that. Lotsa farmers in the area.

Moose Jaw’s kind of a service centre for them.”

“What’s the gravel for?” Nick looked back at the load of stones in the red dump tray.

“Fella’s buildin’ a barn over at Pasqua, east of Moose Jaw. Puttin’ in a cement floor and footings. Not much gravel around the area, so they called on me to haul it down from the quarry near Hanley.”

“Maybe he needs some help moving that gravel to where it needs to go,” Nick said. “Five tons of gravel means a lot of shoveling, and I could sure use the work.”

“Heh heh, you got that right, son. But maybe you don’t need to grab a shovel. If yer a mechanic, I may know a fella who could use you."

"You really think so? Not much available in my line of work these days."

"Guy's name is McKenzie. Got a good little garage right there in Moose Jaw. Does work on my rig when I need it. I'll drop you there, and you can meet him yerself."

They dipped down into the Qu'Appelle Valley, where the trees were in full leaf even though it was only April. Back up on the prairie, the land was still a monochromatic dun colour, with standing water still in some of the fields. It would be three or four weeks yet before tractors could get on the land to plough and seed this year's crop.

McKenzie Mechanical was a few blocks off Main Street, in a brick building with two service bays and two pumps – one for diesel and one for gasoline. Wilf pulled up beside the diesel pump, cut the engine, and set the brakes before hopping down from the cab.

"Oh-h-h, it feels mighty good to stretch," he said, walking around stiff-legged as he worked out the kinks from the long drive. "Howdy, Alex!"

A tall, sandy-haired man looked up from the engine he was working on and smiled.

"Howdy, Wilf," Alex said, coming over and shaking hands. "Been a while."

"Been workin' up around PA hauling fill for a new road," Wilf said.

"What brings you down this way? Any trouble with the rig?"

"Hummin' like a top, Alex. Although, I do need a tankful of diesel. But no, I'm just on my way over to Pasqua with this load of gravel."

"For Wellington White's new barn, I'd guess. It's gonna be a big one. Coffee?"

"Thanks, but no. Just fill up the tank for me, will ya. Pay ya on the way back."

"Look forward to seein' you on the return, then, Wilf." Alex turned and hollered to the kid at the pump. "Hey, Jimmy! Fill up the Mack. Diesel."

"I'm just gonna pop 'round the corner to your facilities, Alex. But Nick, here, is lookin' for work, and I said you might know of some." Wilf stood aside so Alex could get a look at Nick.

"What kinda work you lookin' for?"

"I'm a mechanic, as I was telling Wilf. Worked on trucks up there in Saskatoon, at the Farm Centre out on the highway. Lotta Macks like Wilf's. Jimmys. Also, cars, motorcycles. Bicycles."

"We get a few of those," Alex laughed. "Look, I might be able to use you. We need an extra set of hands here for when I have to go out to service a farmer's machinery in the field. So, you'd have to work unsupervised some of the time. Can you do that?"

"Yes sir," Nick said. "At least, you could put me to the test."

"OK, why don't we give you a trial run. Say a month? Where are you staying?"

"Uh, nowhere, yet. Just got into town."

"Then Auralee'd be good for you. Runs a rooming house over on Cariboo." Nick noted that he pronounced it cara-BOO. "Nice and clean. She feeds you supper, too."

McKenzie Mechanical was hiring because Alexander McKenzie's motto was "Repair Before Replacement." Farmers couldn't afford new equipment during the Depression, so Alex patched up what machinery they had. He was also picking up some work from the Moose Jaw Flying Club, which had recently started a new service, Prairie Airways, flying Beech 18D aircraft out of Rosedale Airport in the northwest part of the city. Pretty soon, Alex was going to need all the help he could get.

Chapter 15

*Ev'ry time it rains, it rains
pennies from heaven.
Don't you know each cloud
contains   pennies   from
heaven?
You'll   find   your   fortune
falling all over town....*

Arthur Johnston

Jenny couldn't get the song out of her head. It was so hopeful, so wistful, and optimistic. Too bad the movie itself was the usual Hollywood dreck, with Bing Crosby playing an ex-con who is thwarted in his plans to become a gondolier in Venice because he has to fulfill a promise. But Jenny thought the music they used in the movie was terrific, and even though she'd heard the song a hundred times, she couldn't get enough of it.

Jenny sold movie tickets at the Allen Theatre, where *Pennies From Heaven* was playing twice a day, three days a week. The twenty-five-cent adult admission price could let people forget their troubles for a few hours and lose themselves in Hollywood romances and adventures. Kids got in for a dime. It was surprising how many people could scrounge up a bit of loose change to go to the movies. The Allen was a grand theatre with more than nine hundred seats and walls covered with *bas relief* images of cavorting cherubs. Jenny's part-time job didn't pay much, but it got her out of the house and into a fantasy world of musicals, drama, cowboys and Indians.

One film in particular got her attention, even though the story was far-fetched as usual. In *Supernatural,* Randolph Scott tries to rescue Carole Lombard, an heiress who is possessed by the soul of a convicted murderer. Jenny was intrigued by the séance portrayed in the movie and wondered if there really was a spirit world, a realm just on the other side of everyday life where the rules were different and reality was more fluid. Buddhists believed it existed, as did some Christians, and the spirit world was very much a part of native North American cultures. But when Jenny mentioned the movie to Michael at home, he dismissed the whole idea with one word.

"Bollocks!" If Michael was an animal, he'd be a bull – obstinate, unyielding, and implacable.

"Won't you even entertain the possibility?"

"If I believe in ghosts, Jenny, then I have to believe in the devil," Michael said, putting down his newspaper for a moment. "And if I believe in the devil, then I have to believe in God, which I don't, despite the best efforts of your mother."

Evangeline Hill was well-named. She was a devout and steadfast evangelist for the Lord who tried to bring her children to God with varying success. Her son, Jacob, was more than willing to accept Christ as his Savior as long as it meant he was in his mother's good graces. Her daughter, Jenny, was not interested in religion in any form, but that didn't stop Evangeline from trying to win her and Michael over to the Lord, making family holiday meals particularly awkward.

"When my mother tries to work on my immortal soul, I just ignore her or laugh at her, and she eventually goes away," Jenny said. "I may not believe in God or the devil, but I have to think there is something more than just... just this." She waved her arm around to include the farm and everything beyond it.

"This," Michael said, looking around, "takes up pretty much all of my time, Jen. I don't have any time or energy for what I can't see."

Sometimes it's better to be married than to be right, so Jenny let the matter drop, and Michael went back to the news story he'd been reading about the death of Moose Jaw fireman Peter Mitchell, who was only 46 years old when he collapsed and died of a heart attack at work. You never knew when

Death was going to come for you until it arrived. His father was only 56 when he was killed by lightning, and his grandfather Hamish was not yet forty. Did the McKenzie Curse on firstborns extend to daughters? Their ten-year-old daughter Amelia was a firstborn, the same as her namesake Amelia Earhart, who vanished last July with her co-pilot while they flew somewhere over the Pacific Ocean near the Equator. Some people thought that the plane may have been struck by lightning. Were some people marked early for death? Were they doomed to live in dread or were they blissfully unaware?

Michael tried to put such errant thoughts out of his head. But what if there was something after all to Jenny's ideas about a spirit world filled with people we loved and lost, who hang around trying to talk to us if only we'd listen. What if his father was hovering around in a parallel world, trying to communicate with his family? Michael had never seen or heard anything to convince him of the existence of such a world, but he'd seen nothing to convince him that it didn't exist either. Thinking about it made his brain hurt because there was no resolution to the idea, no way to prove or disprove the existence of the spirit world. Michael was a practical man. He enjoyed growing crops and working with livestock because they were real. Put a seed in the ground, and it will grow. You could track and measure its progress. This spirit world, what they called the paranormal, was just the opposite – elusive, ephemeral, and unable to be verified. He shook his head, put the whole notion out of his mind, and turned to more practical matters.

The farm was struggling. Michael and Jenny worked all day and often into the evening, but there was never quite enough money to get from one month to the next. Some months, Jenny's wages from the theatre helped keep the place going. Finances were a sore spot for Michael. He was good at farming but bad at financial management, and he knew it. And avoided it. When his brother Scott dropped by one afternoon, the farm's financial problems came into sharp focus.

"The price of wheat is up this year, have I got that right?" Scott asked, to be encouraging. "That's got to feel pretty good." They were sitting at the kitchen table, the focal point for almost all discussions about Home Farm. The place had been awash in red ink since their father's death.

"Forty cents a bushel," Michael said. "Yeah, that's almost twice as much as last year, Scotty. But, twice nothing is still nothing. Last year, I just went broke twice as fast is all. Forty cents this year barely covers my cost of putting the seed in the ground, never mind harvest and storage."

"I don't want to stick my nose in where it's not wanted, Mike, but if you like, I could help you set up a financial planning calendar."

"You gotta have finances to do financial planning," Michael said with a laugh. "We just have bills."

"Maybe there's some money to be saved somewhere along the line," Scott suggested. "I could help you map out a fiscal year, crunch the numbers, and see if there might be some economies."

"Thanks, Scotty, but I'm OK," Michael said. He didn't like to talk about money at all, much less 'finances.'

"It's pretty simple, Mike. We could make a linear chart of your year, and then map the costs and benefits through the fiscal year."

"I don't think of our farm in fiscal years, though Scotty. I think of it as seasons. Calving season. Seeding season. Harvest. Winter." Michael leased Alex and Scott's land from them and had more than a thousand acres in production.

"OK, sure. Then that's the timeline we use, and we can draw up a plan to illustrate that," Scott said. "See where the seasons overlap, see where you could maybe save some money, or where you might be missing marketing opportunities."

"I don't have to market what this farm produces, Scotty. People pay for the quality meat, grain, and hay we sell. I won't compromise that quality." Michael had crossed his arms, signalling that the conversation was over.

"People aren't buying quality these days, Mike. They're buying quantity. If you've got four kids and no job, you're not buying top sirloin, you're buying hamburger and not much of it."

"I know, Scotty, but I can't do it any other way. If I cut corners, stint on the feed or try to get one more calf out of a heifer, I'd be undercutting the quality, so I'd have to lower the price and... you know where that goes."

"What if you could save some money on production without sacrificing quality?"

"Can't be done." Again, the crossed arms and implacable face.

"But will you at least let me show you how I *think* it might work?"

Michael grudgingly agreed and, a few weeks later, was astonished at the result.

"This charts Home Farm's finances for the quarter, from July to September of last year," Scott said, laying out a graph on the kitchen table. "This black line is the farm's income. This red line is your expenses." The black line dipped below the red line more than it rose above it.

"That's what I've been telling you, I just can't seem to make a profit."

Even with low wheat prices, Scott knew there was no way the farm should be losing money. The beef operation alone should have carried the rest of the farm. Michael sold choice cuts to restaurants and high-end butchers in Regina and Saskatoon, who paid top dollar and then charged their customers even more. Rich people didn't seem to suffer too much, even during a Depression. Scott crunched the numbers and came to what proved to be an obvious conclusion.

"Michael, somebody's stealing from you."

"Who? How?" Michael asked in disbelief. He thought the best of everyone and just assumed they'd live up to his expectations. Plus, he only had four or five part-time employees, and none of them got anywhere near the farm's finances.

"I've double-checked the bank deposits, double-checked the payroll, and then triple-checked all that and one thing kinda sticks out."

"What's that? Oh, wait, don't tell me. I know. I'm a bad farmer. Coulda told ya that. But what's this green line above the red and black ones?"

"Remember when Dad died last year?" Scott asked, ignoring his brother's self-deprecation. "And we had to find a manager for the farm until we could sort things out?"

"Yeah. What a relief! Duncan was really a godsend," Michael said. "That calf deal? He stickhandled that while I was still poleaxed by Dad's death."

Robert McKenzie died at the end of the summer of 1935, just as the crops were being harvested and the yearling calves were going to market. Robert's will was a mess and took months to work its way through probate, and, in the meantime, the farm was rudderless. Michael had his hands full with the day-to-day practicalities of getting the crops off the fields. Alex was busy with McKenzie Mechanical, and Scott had his law practice. So, the three brothers hired Duncan McCain to run the place *pro tem* until all the legal details were sorted out. Robert and Duncan were long-time friends, and Duncan had trained Amelia's horse, Blaze, so there was a strong family connection. Once all the legal business had been dealt with, Duncan stayed on to help Michael run the farm.

"Duncan took twenty per cent on that calf deal, Mike. That green line is Duncan's percentage. He takes fifteen to twenty per cent of everything we sell, and he takes it off the top before the cost of production is factored in. Here are the papers to prove it, right out in plain sight if you cared to look. Twenty per cent. Which puts you in the red."

"He said he wouldn't take a salary, just offered to help for a percentage," Mike said. "You know me, Scotty, I'm crap at math. Jenny does all our household finances, or we'd be even more broke than we are."

"Did he say how much of a percentage?"

"I... I thought he said... I mean he didn't really spell it out but..."

"Is there any paperwork? A contract or...?"

"No, just what he called a 'gentlemen's agreement'. A handshake. I just assumed he'd take ten per cent. Isn't that kind of, I don't know, standard? And Scotty, you remember we really needed help, and he was a family friend. He and Dad went 'way back'..." Michael looked out the window for a moment, then turned back to Scott. "Well, hell. Now what?"

"You fire him."

"But who's gonna manage all that buying and selling?"

"It's not that hard, Mike. It was all set up by Dad and in place before Duncan joined us, and it sure as hell shouldn't cost twenty per cent to do the paperwork. I could do it with a little help from Helen at work. You've got a good product. You should be making fifteen per cent profit, not handing it to an employee."

"Fire Duncan, though? He's an old guy."

"He's an old guy who has been cheating you, and if you don't fire him, you're agreeing to be cheated. It'd be cheaper to give him a small annuity than to keep him on, although I don't think he deserves it. He's taken quite a chunk of cash from this farm. What he's done borders on illegal, or at least unethical."

"Will you help me? Fire him? I'm terrible at confrontation." Michael would rather eat bees than give someone bad news.

"You have to do it. You're the one Dad named in the will to manage Home Farm. So, you tell him. I'll draw up a letter to hand him while you're telling him," Scott said. "And I'll be by your side. He can be gone by sundown tomorrow."

Jenny took over the accounting side of the farm business with the help of Scott's financial timeline and budget. Without Duncan McCain siphoning off the profits, the farm was back in the black by the end of the year.

Scott McKenzie had a good reputation as a financial advisor. With his legal skills and financial acumen, he was able to steer farmers through the highs and lows of the markets and help them to understand the increasingly complex tax laws. Part of his skill was optimism. He was able to see possibilities where others saw only problems and roadblocks. At thirty-five, he was hitting his stride. The worst of the Depression and dust bowl days were in the rear-view mirror, his law practice was thriving, and he'd just met Eleanor.

Eleanor Boyko was Scott McKenzie's opposite in every way. He was a three-piece-suit kind of guy; Eleanor wore jeans and a man's plaid shirt. Scott kept in shape by lifting weights, running, and eating well. Ellie ate and drank what she wanted to and smoked Player's Navy Cut because she liked the picture of the old-timey sailor framed by the life ring on the package. She drank endless small cups of strong coffee as she painted all day in a drafty barn on her South Hill property. Scott and Eleanor were chalk and cheese. Silk and sandpaper. So, of course, they were bound to meet.

The scene was a fall supper in Mortlach. The place was packed because the food was always good and plentiful. Particularly popular were the cabbage rolls simmering in tomato sauce made by a few of the local Ukrainian ladies. Eleanor and Scott reached for the serving spoon at the same time, and their hands touched.

"Go ahead," Scott said gallantly, withdrawing his hand. Ceding the floor to a beautiful woman was always a good call.

"These are the best *holubtsi* I ever ate," Eleanor said as she scooped up four plump cabbage rolls and plopped them on her plate.

"Ukrainian?" Scott asked.

"*Tak ukrayins'ka,*" she answered with a smile. "We're big eaters. I'm Eleanor. Ellie. And you?" She took another big spoonful of cabbage rolls and dumped them on Scott's plate.

"Uh, I'm Scott. Scotty," he mumbled. "Thanks." He wasn't usually at a loss for words, but somehow his mouth had gone dry, and his tongue was twice its normal size.

"Where are you sitting?"

"Nowhere."

"Hey, Scotty, everybody's gotta be somewhere," she said out of the side of her mouth like a gangster. "Come, sit with us."

And so, Scott Mckenzie, buttoned-down barrister at law, met and married into the boisterous Boyko bunch, a plunge into ice cold water that took his breath away. The constant conversations, crosstalk, asides, short skits, arguments, and general shenanigans exhausted him. He couldn't keep up with the eating and drinking, and Ellie advised him not to try.

"It's not a competition, dear man," she said, nuzzling his neck. "It's a dance."

Chapter 16

Like fat mechanical bees, dozens of yellow Harvard aircraft droned back and forth above Moose Jaw as hundreds of young men learned to fly in anticipation of war breaking out in Europe. The Harvard had such a slow stall speed that it was almost impossible to crash, hence its popularity with the Royal Air Force training base just south of Moose Jaw and the one fifteen miles west at Caron. Despite stiff winds and the occasional thunderstorm, the prairies were ideal for training pilots because there was so little to crash into, although some pilots were injured or killed in 'hard landings' – coming in too fast or hitting the brakes in panic and flipping the aircraft on its nose.

Alexander McKenzie was thirty-eight years old, and while he'd registered for the army, he doubted he'd be called up unless they were desperate. They wanted physically fit young men, not beefy, middle-aged guys like him. So, while the world prepared for war, Alex built his business. McKenzie Mechanical had three service bays now, as well as a tow truck and experienced mechanics who could go out on calls. Alex still took care of the equipment at Home

Farm, which was now run exclusively by Michael and Jenny with help from their daughter Amelia, who was almost a teenager. But, otherwise, Alex devoted all his time to his business.

One morning in May of 1939, he got a telephone call at work from a man with a clipped British accent. He introduced himself as Flying Officer Reginald H. Cross and wasted no time getting to the point.

"Mr. McKenzie, we need you out here at 1400 hours today. The briefing will last two hours," Cross said. Alex imagined him to be a small man with a tortured little moustache.

"Briefing? For what?"

"Classified, sir."

"Which means you can't tell me."

"Correct, sir."

"And 1400 hours... that's, what, two pm?"

"Correct."

"That's in three hours. Sorry, but I've got my hands full here for the rest of the day." That was an understatement. The rest of the week was more like it. Alex looked around at the three cars up on the hoists, three more vehicles parked outside the service bays, waiting their turn, and another five or six parked on the other side of the gas pumps for tomorrow or the next day. Like a hospital Emergency Room, Alex triaged the cars according to whether they required a quick fix, an overhaul, or a rebuild due to a case of chronic neglect. He'd also been servicing some of the little Tiger Moths and Beechcrafts kept at the airport north of town run by the Moose Jaw Flying Club and had to hire two more mechanics to manage the workload.

Finally, after a decade of hard times, things were starting to pick up again. There were still more than a million Canadians without a job, but the worst seemed to be over, except even in the sweet, hopeful spring of 1939, there was talk of a war in Europe. Flying Officer Cross was barking something important down the phone line, so Alex stopped daydreaming and tuned back in.

"Exigencies notwithstanding, that's as may be," Cross was saying. "This takes priority. A matter of national urgency and security." He sounded serious, as in call out the troops serious, so Alex thought he should play along.

"Okay. I'll... I'll be there," Alex said. Maybe this was his call-up. Prime Minister Mackenzie King was holding off on conscription for fear of alienating Quebec voters, but he had the threat in his back pocket should the need arise. There was still hope peace would prevail, although every sign pointed to war.

"Hey, Nick, can you c'mere for a sec?" Alex hollered across the service bays after hanging up the phone.

"What's up, boss?" Nick Rizzo asked, wiping his hands on an oily rag. "Got that Hudson ready to go in Bay Two, so maybe we can bring in the Nash? That'll be a quickie." Nick had been working at McKenzie Mechanical for almost three years and had settled into the job like he'd always done it. He was unflappably pleasant and polite, even with the most demanding customers. Return business was up, and the shop was busier than ever.

"I gotta go out to the base this afternoon, Nick. Can you keep an eye on things here?"

"You bet. Say, someone came by looking for work, so I said I'd ask you. Anything going?"

"Does he know a crescent wrench from a crowbar?"

"She."

"Who?"

"The guy. Looking for work. It's a woman. Name's KD."

"KD? What's that stand for?"

"Didn't ask."

"And she knows how to fix cars?"

"Had her look at that Studebaker, and she told me what was wrong inside a minute. Then she told me how she'd fix it, and she was right on the money, Alex."

"Well, what do you think?" Alex was giving Nick more say in the running of the business, and he was stepping up to the task.

"Just from talking to her, I think she may know what she's doing. She seems to know a camshaft from a carburetor. She was right about that Studebaker. And we could use an extra set of hands."

"OK, let's try her out. Put her on with Bruno, see how she does." What Bruno Czarda didn't know about engines wasn't worth knowing. He'd run his own shop for more than a decade but didn't want the headaches of managing a business anymore, so he brought his customers to McKenzie, where he was quite content to work as a mechanic for wages and predictable hours.

"Sure. And don't worry. We got you covered, boss. Take as much time as you need." Nick smiled and went back to the head gasket he was installing on a 1935 DeSoto.

Alex went home, showered, and put on a clean shirt, still trying to figure out why an RAF officer would want to meet with him. If he was going to be drafted, he'd get a letter in the mail from the Canadian army, not the Brits. He drove south on the highway for a few miles, then took the road to the air base. The fields south of town were greening up nicely while overhead half a dozen yellow Harvards droned across the sky in formation. He pulled up beside the CO's office on the base and went inside where he introduced himself to the Staff Sergeant at the front desk. It was ten minutes before two pm. The Staff Sergeant made a call, muttered a few words, and hung up. From down the hallway Alex heard a scolding voice coming closer.

"There is NEVER an excuse for that sort of behaviour, Corporal, and in future – *if* you have a future here that is – you would be well advised to remember that."

A tall, thin, clean-shaven soldier with gold braid on his hat and medals on his chest came striding into the reception area as the Staff Sergeant on the desk snapped to attention and saluted. The chastised Corporal was nowhere to be seen.

"I'm Flying Officer Cross, Mr. McKenzie," the soldier said, shaking Alex's hand. "How good of you to come. You're a bit early, which is a good sign. We're in the conference room. Please join us." He turned smartly and strode down the long hall. Alex followed. Halfway down, a doorway led them into a big boxy room furnished with trestle tables and folding chairs occupied by half a dozen uniformed officers. At the front of the room was a large blackboard on a wheeled stand.

"Gentlemen," said F/O Cross. "This is Alexander McKenzie, the man I told you about. Mr. McKenzie, these men are looking for someone to run their motor pool, and by motor pool, I mean aeroplanes."

"I don't know much about airplanes, sir," Alex said.

"The Moose Jaw Flying Club would beg to disagree. They say you are adept at diagnosing and fixing their Beech 18D aeroplane engines, which use a Pratt and Whitney R-985 engine. Our Harvard trainers use a Pratty and Whitney R-1340 – remarkably similar. Both have a slow stall speed and feature reliable handling at low altitude."

"I don't know about any of that, sir. Pratt and Whitney make a good engine, but I..."

"McKenzie Mechanical is not unknown to us here. You are regarded as a capable manager of men. You have a staff of...?"

"Eleven, including three part-time."

"I'll come to the point, Mr. McKenzie. We need a man who can ride herd on a motor pool of about a dozen men tasked with maintaining our aeroplanes. You are familiar with the engines, and you know how to run a team. At this moment, there is no one in our ranks who fits that description, hence our telephone call to you. If you are up to the challenge, I will confer upon you the rank of Pilot Officer for the duration."

"The duration of what, sir? I mean, thank you, sir, I think, but how long is the duration? As I mentioned, I have a business..."

"War, Mr. McKenzie. In Europe. By Christmas at the very latest. We need to train hundreds of pilots in a very short time. And we need reliable aircraft with which to train them. So, I am recruiting you to run the motor pool here, to turn a dozen disparate mechanics into a reliable team. For the duration of what will most certainly be a war. It's literally a life-and-death situation. Our pilots must be able to trust their aircraft absolutely and without hesitation. And they must have faith in the people who maintain them because up there, it's the pilot's life on the line."

Alex looked around the room. Like F/O Cross, the men all had gold braid on their hats, medals on their chests, and gray in what hair they had left. They had no doubt fought in the Great War, and now were being asked once again to do their duty.

"I very much doubt, sir, that I am up to the job you're asking me to do," Alex said before he could think about it too long. "But I will give it my best and hope that your trust in me is not misplaced."

"Glad to hear it, young man. Of course, you will have to sign the Official Secrets Act and swear allegiance to the King. Are you prepared to do that?"

"I guess so. I mean, yes, sir."

"Then I hereby appoint you, Pilot Officer First Class, in His Majesty's Royal Air Force." He saluted smartly, and Alex instinctively saluted back.

Alex spent the next several hours filling in forms, swearing oaths, getting briefed and debriefed, and measured for the uniform of an officer in the Royal Air Force. Sometime before day turned to night, he telephoned the garage and talked with Nick.

"You OK to run things for a while?" Alex asked.

"You goin' to war, boss?"

"Just here on the base. Fixing airplanes. I'll explain when I see you tomorrow, but I thought I should give you a heads up. And a chance to say no."

"I'm on deck here boss, as long as you need me. Or until they call me up at least."

"If they do, I'll make sure you get assigned to my motor pool out here."

"Thanks boss."

Chapter 17

*I remember the night and
the Tennessee Waltz
Now I know just how much
I have lost
Yes, I lost my little darling
the night they were playing
The beautiful Tennessee
Waltz...*

Pee Wee King

Her voice was like nothing he'd ever heard – lonesome and heartbroken but wise. And womanly, pitched low, and natural. His knuckles were raised to rap on the door of Number 53, but he waited, frozen, entranced by the music coming from inside. The singing ended, but the guitar kept playing for a chorus, solid flat-picking for an old-timey country waltz. When the music stopped completely, Nick almost applauded but knocked instead.

The National Motel was not likely to be featured on any picture postcards sent home with the message: *Having wonderful time. Wish you were here.* The National was where road crews stayed, where truckers could park their rig right along the highway and grab four hours of sleep to keep their logbook up to date. It was the kind of accommodation where travelling salesmen slept next to their sample boxes. But it was cheap and cheerful, and the showers were hot. Nick knocked again. Right after Alex called, Nick decided to offer KD the mechanic's job, so he went over to where she was staying to tell her the good news.

The door to Number 53 opened a crack to reveal a boy's face looking up at him. Across the room, a woman sat on the couch, cradling a guitar. She smiled, laid the guitar aside, came over, and opened the door wider.

"Hi," she said. "Nick, right? This is my boy, Robert. He's ten. We call him Bobby," KD said with a smile that just couldn't seem to help itself. She kept grinning, like she was happy to be here. Or anywhere.

"Hi," said Bobby, sticking out a hand to shake. He had the same open face as his mother, with a spray of freckles across his nose and reddish hair that hadn't seen a brush for a while. Not much of a smile, though. More of a wary glare. Protective of his mom.

"Say, have you got a minute?" Nick asked KD, while shaking the boy's hand. "I'm not interrupting...?"

"No. Sure. Come on in," she said, standing aside.

"Maybe..."

"Bobby's fine. His daddy left us in '38, so it's just Bobby and me. We've been kinda rootless ever since looking for a place to settle, so he's in on everything I do. Come on in. Take a pew."

The tidy room had two beds, a couch, and a couple of straight-backed chairs. A good Crosley radio sat on top of a small icebox, and there was a hot plate, a sink, and a few cupboards for food. Nick sat in one of the kitchen chairs while KD curled up like a cat on the couch, and Bobby hovered.

"Look, I'll just come out and say it," Nick began. "We... that is, Mr. McKenzie and I think that..."

"It's OK," she said, looking at Bobby. Her smile drooped a bit, but it was still there. "I understand. We'd hoped Moose Jaw could be a place we could settle down, but I guess a girl mechanic isn't..."

"You got the job if you want it," Nick interrupted. "Start Monday. Or tomorrow, if you like. Eight am. We got a lot of work."

KD looked surprised then quietly hugged Robert who almost cracked a smile.

"Really?" she said. "'Cuz I will start tomorrow, if y'all need me to. I got some of my own tools too, though you prob'ly have some too... I talk too much don't I?"

"You talk just fine, but what happens to...?" Nick wasn't sure it was any of his business.

"Bobby? He goes to school down the street, then comes back here and does his homework. Doesn't he?" She looked at Bobby, who blushed.

"Sorry. None of my..."

"Hey, you can ask. I would. You don't know us from a hole in the ground. But thank you. For the job. I'll be there tomorrow morning, eight sharp. You gotta know you made my day. Our day."

"Well, I, uh... I'll let you get back to... I just wanted..."

"See you tomorrow, Mr. Rizzo."

"Nick. It's Nick."

"KD, but you know that. Short for Kitty Dawn, which sounds like a bur-lee-cue queen or something, don't it? Who'd ever name their kid Kitty Dawn, I ask ya? Sorry. Talkin' too much again. My mother calls it 'oversharing' or something." She shrugged and threw her hands up in mock despair.

Nick looked at her hands for the first time. At the shop, he was too busy assessing her mechanical skills to wonder about her hands. But now that he had time to look at them, he wondered how they could make such beautiful music come out of a guitar. They were short and pudgy, with scraped knuckles and ingrained grease under the stubby nails. Not beautiful hands at all. The hands of a grease monkey, not a musician.

"That music, when I knocked on the door..."

"Yeah?"

"Was that you?"

"Yeah. Pretty hokey, eh?"

"You have the sweetest voice I've ever heard," Nick said before he could stop himself. "And how in heck do you play guitar with..."

"These old things?" she laughed and twiddled her grubby fingers. "Hey, Andrés Segovia has pudgy fingers, and look what he can do with 'em."

"Who's Andrés...?"

"Segovia. Pretty good classical guitarist with small hands."

"But how come you're fixing cars? Shouldn't you be playing music in a theatre or something?"

"Used to, as it happens. But then..."

"What happened? Oh, sorry. Didn't mean to..."

"That's OK. Bobby's daddy and I were a fairly good team. I sang and played guitar and Freddy sang and played fiddle. We worked around Toronto for quite a few years, then times got hard and people stopped paying to go hear music. Then, Freddy stopped playing fiddle with me and started to fiddle around... elsewhere, you might say. Playing away. But there I go, oversharing again. You don't wanna know all this."

"So, you and Bobby have been on your own for two years?"

"Guess so, eh Bobby?"

"We do OK," Bobby said, ducking his head.

"Man, that's a long time, especially for a kid. I may know of a furnished house in town that's for rent. Would you be interested?"

"You bet I would. If I have the job, that is."

"Oh, you've got the job, although I might just pay you to play music all day."

"Don't think you'd get your money's worth," KD said and laughed.

"OK, then," Nick said, getting to his feet. "Guess I better get out of your hair." He got up and walked over to the door. He wanted to stay and talk more with KD, maybe hear her play some more, but he didn't want to get too personal. Emotions were best left off the shop floor.

"See y'all tomorrow. And thanks again," KD said, closing the door behind him.

As Nick climbed into his truck, he thought he heard whoops and hollers coming from Number 53.

Chapter 18

Amelia McKenzie sat on the cool granite step in front of the Girls Entrance to Ross School and screwed up her courage to go inside. She was twelve years old and going into Grade Six, the top of the school pecking order. She learned about pecking orders from her father Michael, when he told her how she could earn a little extra allowance by taking care of the chickens.

"See that rooster over there?" he asked her, pointing out a strutting Rhode Island Red. "He is quite literally the cock of the walk in this barnyard, the top of the pecking order. There are other roosters, but he's tougher and bigger than they are. They give him lots of room, and so should you. Get too close and he'll come at you with those sharp spurs on his legs, 'cause he is all about protecting the hens. And that hen over there? Whaddya see?"

"She looks kinda beat up," Amelia said. "Or sick. Does she need protection?"

"She doesn't get any because she's at the bottom of the pecking order in this particular henhouse. If she goes anywhere near the rooster, the other hens will attack her."

"Why? What'd she do?"

"She's just the weakest, that's all," Michael said kindly. "So, they keep her from having chicks. It's nature's way of choosing the best and strongest strain to continue the line."

"But isn't it cruel to leave her there all beat up? You could take her out of there."

"Sure. But then they'd just select the next weakest hen and attack her."

"That's unfair."

"It isn't fair or unfair. It just *is*," Michael said. "It's the way of most things."

Amelia knew she didn't want to be the weakest hen. She also knew she would have to fight for her place because of what had happened over the summer.

It started innocently enough with a chance comment her mother made to Agnes Randolph, that grumpy woman who ran the Ladies Auxiliary at the church. Amelia's parents didn't go to church, which in itself was a social crime. But then, at a school bake sale, her mom started talking about a movie she'd seen a while back about ghosts and the paranormal.

"It was called *Supernatural*," Jenny told Agnes. "Randolph Scott tries to rescue Carole Lombard, who's been taken over by the spirit of a murderess. There was a scene with a séance which..."

"What sort of nonsense are you talking about?" asked Agnes.

"What nonsense? It's just a movie," Jenny laughed. "You know, entertainment?"

"Filling your head with that sort of thing, yet I never see you in church. It's no wonder 'why' you believe in the devil." Agnes Randolph scowled and turned on her heel. She was soon across the gymnasium floor, talking to a clutch of three ladies in print dresses who were looking back at Jenny and Amelia.

Over the next few weeks, the whispers spread like a prairie wildfire as Agnes and her righteous circle of friends told anyone who would listen about the evil that lived among them. The McKenzies worshipped the devil, it was said, and as a reward were permitted Satanic powers of second sight. Like Verlane Dupray and her once-innocent daughter Alice, Jennifer McKenzie had gone to the dark side and taken her husband Michael and their daughter Amelia with her. The child was corrupted by her depraved parents and was beyond reach. As if God didn't have enough to do, He saw fit to rain lightning down on Michael's father and grandfather, both firstborns and deserving of the bolts. The McKenzie Curse, they called it. Agnes Randolph made sure everyone knew about the McKenzie Curse.

Amelia went to an art class in Crescent Park in early July. The sun was beating down, and it was hot even where they painted in the shade of a couple of towering cottonwoods. Her friend, Betty-Ann Trask, turned from her work and smiled sweetly at Amelia. They'd known each other since Grade Three.

"Can't you do some kind of spell to cool things down?" Betty-Ann asked. Nancy Engel and a girl in glasses, whose name Amelia didn't know, smirked and tittered.

"Spell?"

"Well, you know, like your mom."

"What are you talking about, Betty-Ann?"

"She doesn't want to come right out and say that your mom is a witch," said Nancy, at her easel next to Betty-Ann. "But I will. My mother says your mother is in league with the devil himself."

"You're a witch, too. Everyone knows about you, Camelia," said the girl in glasses.

"Some of them even know my name. It's *Amelia*," she said. "And why do you think my mother is a witch?"

"Tough question," Betty-Ann said, emboldened now by her supporters. "Let's see, is it because she believes all those superstitions and thinks she controls the lightning? Or maybe because she worships the devil?"

"Yeah," said the girl in glasses. "Your mother loves Satan."

"Shhhhh!" said Nancy and Betty-Ann in unison, crossing themselves. "Don't say the name. It's bad luck." The girl in glasses shrank under their disapproval.

"Now who's being superstitious?" Amelia asked. She packed her paints, rolled up her canvas, folded her easel and left the park.

"Now who's being superstitious?" Nancy mocked in a sneering sing-song voice.

"Stupid-stitious," said the girl in the glasses, to withering glances from Nancy and Betty-Ann.

Amelia spent the rest of the summer on her own, which she found surprisingly enjoyable. Both her parents worked all day, so she helped out with chores around Home Farm and then spent the rest of the day either walking through the countryside or reading on the porch. But all summer, she kept thinking that September would come sooner or later, school would begin, and she'd have to find a way to handle the savage gossip of elementary school. Now, here she sat on the step like a silly girl afraid to face the music instead of going in with her head held high like a mature Grade Six. She got up, brushed off her pleated knee-length skirt, and went inside.

The familiar school smells of chalk and apple cores hung in the hallways that were choked with kids as Amelia navigated her way like a salmon swimming upstream. Nobody looked at her when she entered her classroom. Nobody spoke to her as she chose an empty desk and sat down.

Everyone's eyes were focused on the one word written on the blackboard in big capital letters:

WAR

Chapter 19

Alberta may be the coldest province in Canada, but Saskatchewan consistently gives it a run for the title. And the winter of 1939-40 was one for the record books. The first snow was in early November, and it snowed heavily a dozen times more. The temperature rarely got above zero, so the snow was piled higher and higher until the big melt in late April.

'Six months of winter and two months of poor sledding' is the way Danny Siggelow characterized the weather in Moose Jaw. Such a difference from Moncton, where any day below zero was considered brutally cold. Of course, the wind and moisture off the Atlantic often made it feel colder, but it was nothing like a Saskatchewan winter, where ten below was balmy, especially if there was no wind.

When Saskatchewan warms up, it does so in a hurry. By April, streams crowd their banks, steam rises from the thawing soil, and people emerge from their houses in shorts and tee shirts ready to dig in the garden. But they would be unwise to do so. There are unwritten rules, and those who ignore them pay the price. One of those rules is that nothing goes into the ground before Queen Victoria's birthday on the 24th of May.

"Don't put those seeds in the ground just yet," Alice cautioned Siggy in early May, just as she had the year before. "Any time before the 24th, and you'll have to plant them again."

"May 24th? It's seventy degrees out there right now. Even if I plant today, we won't get much out of the garden until half past August. It's such a short season here."

"Better than getting nothing at all," Alice laughed. "It feels warm now, but May can bring frosty nights and even snow. Your tender seedlings wouldn't stand a chance. My dad lost eleven head of cattle and calves one spring when a snowstorm came blowing out of Alberta, May 15th,

and it buried them alive, the calves still at their momma's side, frozen. Even Dad didn't see that coming."

Arthur Dupray was legendary for being able to predict the annual change to warm weather to the precise day, much like Alice's mother could predict lightning. Siggy didn't put much stock in such beliefs, but Arthur was rarely wrong, and Verlane was uncannily correct on most of her predictions. Alice, too, had some kind of sixth sense that even she couldn't understand, but that allowed her to know a kind of future. Siggy liked to kid her about it.

"Ooooh!" he would cry in mock alarm. "The baby's gonna be hungry when he wakes up. I can just feel it in my bones."

"Joke all you like, Danny boy," she said. "But go see what that son of yours wants." The sound of a fussing baby came from an upstairs bedroom.

"Sure, AJ's my son when he wants something or needs his diaper changed," Siggy joked, but he went willingly. AJ (Arthur for Alice's father and Jasper for Danny's father) was seven months old, born just as war broke out in Europe. Who plans their life around war? Siggy thought he should do his patriotic duty by enlisting in the army, but Alice convinced him not to.

"You've got a baby to take care of," she said. "And you work on the railroad, which is an essential service during wartime."

"Yeah, but maybe I could help, you know, over there."

"Well, I didn't want to say this, but you're also getting a little long in the tooth for going 'over there.' Let the young men fight the war."

"Thirty-three ain't long in the tooth. Anyway, you're older than me."

"Not by much, and I'm not the one talking about going to war, am I? We want you here, Danny boy. Alive. Healthy. You're a husband and a father. We *need* you here."

Alice melted him with her smile, and all thoughts of a military career were forgotten until June 21, 1940, when the National

Resources Mobilization Act was passed into law by Mackenzie King's Liberal government. All able-bodied men between the ages of 20 and 45 had to register with the military authorities and were eligible for call-up for the duration of the war. Unlike the 1918 anti-conscription riots in Montreal, there was little opposition to the legislation this time, except, again, in Quebec. Like most other Canadian men of a certain age, Siggy signed up to do his duty and waited for the call.

While he waited, he got on with his life, working at the railroad and spending as much time as possible with his little family. The summer rolled on, and life was sweet. Siggy loved having a son and looked forward to teaching him how to grow up to be a man, how to grow food and hunt for game, to ride a bike or run for a long pass. His own father had been away most of the time, working on the fishing boats in the Northumberland Strait or just wandering the Maritimes looking for work, leaving Siggy's mother and his two sisters to scrabble for a living. As soon as he finished school, Siggy headed west to find steady work and still sent money home every month.

"Letter for you, toots," she hollered down the hall. "Looks important."

"Be there in a sec," he called back as he fit the new faucet onto the kitchen sink. One faucet instead of two, so now they could have a mix of hot and cold water with the touch of one tap. It was a simple fix, but one that had been bugging him since they moved into the house last summer, just before AJ was born. Another job to scratch off the to-do list, which was now only sixty pages long.

"This looks serious, Danny boy," Alice said when she handed him the letter. *Canadian Army* was part of the cancellation mark on the stamp, and it was addressed to Daniel Jonathon Siggelow. It's never a good sign when they use all three of your names. Siggy slit open the envelope with his thumb and pulled out the letter inside. So much for the to-do list.

"Says I have to report to the Army, Monday, October 10th," Siggy said after reading the short letter a second time. October 10th, three days before AJ's first birthday.

"Are you going to?" Alice asked.

"I *have* to," Siggy said.

"You could say no. Be a conscientious objector or something. Aren't you an essential worker on the railway?"

"But I *have* to go. I can't *not* go. I couldn't live with myself, hon."

"It's Europe's war, not ours. I don't want to lose you."

"No chance of that," he said. "But I gotta do this. I knew it before conscription came in, and I sure as hell know it now. And don't you worry. I'll come back as soon as I can.

As soon as they let me. Your mom can help with AJ, can't she?"

"But she's not you. You'll be off killing strangers on another continent for who knows how long, and AJ will be growing up without his father. What does 'the duration' mean anyway? That's all I ever hear. It's for 'the duration.' How the hell long is that? And how come *you* have to go?"

"You know I've been feeling bad all summer about not enlisting. People look at me as if to say, why aren't you in uniform? I couldn't live with myself, couldn't look you or AJ in the face if I don't go now."

"I knew you'd say that," Alice said, smiling her cat smile. "Because I know my husband. And I love my husband. So, I got you this."

Siggy took the little package she handed him, peeled off the blue wrapping paper, and opened the brown box. Nestled inside was the red vulcanized rubber handle of a Swiss Army knife with half a dozen attachments, including two carbon steel blades, a screwdriver, scissors, a bottle opener, and a corkscrew.

"In case you have to open a bottle of French wine for some *femme fatale* spy," Alice said.

"You are the best," Siggy said, wrapping Alice in a full-on bear hug. "And I will come back. That I promise you."

Chapter 20

*So will you please say hello
to the folks that I know. Tell
them I won't be long.
They'll be happy to know
that as you saw me go, I
was singing this song.*

*We'll meet again, don't
know where, don't know
when. But I know we'll meet
again some sunny day...*

Vera Lynn

Work in the shop slowed down for a moment or two as Vera Lynn and an Air Force choir sang on the radio. When the song was over, the clamour and banging resumed as a dozen men went back to work on half a dozen Harvard aircraft. One of the young mechanics hesitated for a moment and then walked over to Pilot Officer Alexander McKenzie.

"Sir, it's making that noise again." Cpl. Billy Treger looked hopeful, as if Alex had all the answers. In this case, he did. But he made Treger work for it.

"What noise is that, Corporal?" he asked.

"You know, sir, the droning noise."

"That's what they sound like, Mr. Treger. Harvards, I mean."

"But it sounds like it's gonna stall out or blow up, I don't know which."

"I'll let you in on a little secret," Alex said. "It's a sonic boom."

"But... it's a Harvard! You have to exceed Mach I to make a sonic boom. You couldn't do Mach I in a Harvard. Could you, sir?"

"It's not the aircraft itself, Corporal. The B11 has a short propeller, does it not, that revolves rather quickly. So, what you're hearing is the wind around the prop tips, exceeding Mach I."

"Really?"

"Really. Now, what's the story on those aileron balance tabs on 386?"

Alex was working flat out and still unable to meet the demand for airworthy planes that could be used to teach young pilots the rudiments of flying. The attrition rate was frightening – more than half the RCAF pilots sent overseas were killed in action, and many more were wounded or taken prisoner. Operation Chastise was one of the most audacious campaigns and involved a couple of boys from Moose Jaw. Flying great lumbering Lancaster bombers at 240 mph just sixty feet above the targets, the men of 617 Squadron took out three dams critical to the German war effort using five-ton cylindrical bombs that bounced across the water and into the concrete structures to inflict maximum damage. The 'Dambusters' suffered terrible losses – eight Lancasters and fifty-three air crew. Sgt. Pilot Ken Brown made it back home to Moose Jaw, where he'd done his first training. Robert 'Turk' Urquhart did not come home. He was twenty-three years old when his Lancaster was shot down on May 17, 1943 over Emmerich am Rhein, Germany, killing all seven crew members. These young men, most of them in their twenties, knew the odds they faced, yet they went willingly, eagerly, because they knew the alternative if Hitler and the Axis powers prevailed. So, it was critical that Alex and his crew keep the training aircraft flying, even as he worried that he was helping to send some of these men to their deaths.

The British Commonwealth Air Training Program (BCATP) was a joint show between the RAF and the RCAF, using the slow, lumbering Harvards to train pilots at Moose Jaw and Caronport, where the flat and forgiving prairie stretched for mile after unbroken mile. The Harvard 11B was almost crash-proof, a sturdy workhorse with a cruising speed of 140 mph and a range of 700 miles. You could land one in a field if absolutely necessary, and sometimes it was. The planes suffered a lot of wear and tear, and it was P/O McKenzie's job to command the crew of mechanics that kept the kites in the air.

"Sir, the ailerons can be used in the fixed position as trim tabs, but it's the left rudder that's the problem. It only goes fifteen degrees when it needs to go twice that."

"It's not a sticky cable that's the problem because you've already checked that." The Socratic method.

"Yes, sir. No, sir, it's not a sticky cable. We checked. It's the control itself. I think."

"Let's have a look." The two men walked out of the hangar to where a rank of yellow Harvard aircraft sat in various stages of undress as the heat shimmered across the tarmac. Some of the planes had the cowling off and the engine disassembled. Others were getting patches on their fuselage or new landing gear or touchups to the bright yellow paint on the prop tips. They found 386 and Cpl. Treger climbed up into the cockpit to work the rudder control while P/O McKenzie looked at the rudder itself, a moveable flap on the trailing edge of the tail.

"Looks OK from here," he hollered back up to Treger.

"They only notice it in flight, sir," Treger hollered back.

Alex walked back up to the cockpit and climbed up the wing to talk to Treger.

"So, why does it fail in flight when it works fine on the ground?"

"Because of the wind, sir? More pressure from the wind?"

"Is that a question or an answer?"

"An answer, sir. The wind."

"Got it in one, Corporal. Well done. So, what's the solution?"

"Strengthen the linkage so there's more control."

"I think so too. Would you and Cpl. Lindstrom work on that this morning, then we can see how it works in flight this afternoon." He had the mechanics working in two-man teams, which was the most efficient use of manpower. He could use another dozen mechanics, but they were in short supply.

Alex learned how to fly during his first six months on the job, reasoning that if he was going to keep the planes flying, he had to know how they worked in the air, how they handled, and how the controls felt. If he was going to carry the rank of Pilot Officer, he should at least be a pilot.

"What does the forecast say, Willy?" he asked Flight Sergeant William Tremblay when he got to the control tower. It was a stubby little tower but quite serviceable for a prairie airport.

"Five by five, sir," Willy said, using the old radio lingo. "Clear as a bell and not a cloud in sight."

"Wind?"

"There's always wind, sir, but today it's light. Out of the northwest at four miles an hour."

"So, can we take 386 up after lunch? Just a test hop, maybe half an hour?"

"Yeah, we got classes at noon and again at two, so you should be good. Most of them are going northwest on runway one into the breeze, so I'll send you south on two."

Alex went to the canteen for a sandwich and a cup of what passed for coffee on the base, then got into his flight suit and met Cpl. Treger back on the tarmac beside 386.

"She juiced up?" he asked.

"Good to go, sir. A hundred and ten gallons of the best. All we need is a quick instrument check when she's running and you're off."

Five minutes later, Alex slid the canopy shut, adjusted his oxygen mask, and turned the aircraft to taxi south down the runway. The left rudder was a little stiff, but it was easy enough to control the plane as it gathered speed, and within a minute, he was airborne. He climbed to 4,000 feet and levelled off at 130 mph while he tried the left rudder, moving it back and forth so that the aircraft sashayed through the skies like a fan dancer. He turned 180 degrees and tried the same maneuver heading into the light wind, and again the plane behaved as it should, meaning that Treger and Lindstrom had done their job.

Alex didn't enjoy being a boss, which may be why he was good at his job. He'd always been able to think through a mechanical problem, to work on the possibilities until he'd narrowed down the cause to one thing, which he then fixed. He liked to talk things through with the air crews and mechanics, to better understand how they solved problems, then test-fly the aircraft himself if necessary to get to the root of the problem. After another 180, he set a heading for the base. And that's when all his instruments failed – airspeed, altitude, trim, direction – all the needles flat, blank, motionless.

"386 to base. 386 to base. Can you read me?" Alex spoke into the mask without much hope of a response. There was no sound in his headphones, and it seemed like the entire electrical system of the plane was fried. He looked down at the patchwork of farms to identify familiar landmarks while executing a long, slow turn to lose altitude. He could see Thunder Creek where it joined the Moose Jaw River, so he followed the river southwest toward the base. With no altimeter or gyroscope, he'd have to do a seat-of-the-pants landing while trying to judge how far he was above the deck. But he never got that far.

A buzzing blue light welded his hands to the stick as he tried to control the plane's pitch and yaw. The whole cockpit was sizzling, electric. Alex couldn't get a breath, couldn't focus his eyes or free his hands from the controls, much less move them. The Harvard droned ever louder, the only sound in the sky until it augured into a field of wheat half a mile shy of the runway.

Emergency crews arrived within minutes to find Alex dead in the cockpit with no sign that he'd tried to eject or use his parachute. The plane's peeled and buckled yellow paint gave off acrid wisps of smoke. The reinforced rudder was still intact.

Chapter 21

"Are you gonna change the name?" Michael asked.

"Yeah. Something snazzy like Rizzo's Rest or maybe just Nick's like Rick's in *Casablanca* – everybody comes to Nick's," Scott said with a laugh.

"Wouldn't dream of it, you guys. The name *is* the business. What the ad men call brand identification. People come here *because* it's McKenzie Mechanical. They trust this place to take good care of their machines."

Nick Rizzo was on top of the world. He and the two brothers were discussing the purchase of McKenzie Mechanical from Alex's estate. While Alex worked full time maintaining the squadron of Harvards in his care, Nick ran McKenzie Mechanical. When Alex died, Scott and Michael asked Nick to continue managing the garage while they decided what to do with the place. It was Scott who suggested that Nick buy the business, and although Nick felt a little ghoulish that he might be profiting from a man's death, the timing was perfect.

When Alex went to work on the base, Nick had been so busy he sometimes slept at the garage to be there when the first customer came in at the crack of dawn to drop off their broken automobile. Then things got serious with KD. He tried not to fall in love with her because they worked together, but it was because they worked together that he fell in love. He just liked being around her. She was easy to be with – sunny, capable, cute, and funny. She cracked jokes that would make a sailor blush. And she sang like an angel. Plus, she was a good mechanic. He couldn't *not* fall in love with her. His mind still drifted away when he thought of her, so he pulled himself back and concentrated on what Michael was saying.

"They finally sent us the autopsy report on Alex," he said. "It was dark lightning that hit the aircraft."

"What?" Nick looked from Michael to Scott and back again in disbelief. "I thought the airplane crapped out on him," he said.

"It did," said Scotty, "because the gauges and controls were fried by dark lightning. At least, that's what they told us."

"What the hell is 'dark' lightning, anyway? Doesn't lightning usually come with a flash or something?"

"This stuff is so fast it's invisible."

"Wait, invisible? Now there's invisible lightning? This world is getting too wacky."

"That's what they told us," Scotty said.

"They" were a military tribunal charged with determining the cause of air crashes. They were understandably busy these days, what with the war and all, so it took them several months to review the reports and come up with a ruling, then it was another month before anyone thought to tell the McKenzie family. The tribunal ruled out pilot error and found that the cause of the crash was equipment failure due to the aircraft being struck by dark lightning – a terrestrial gamma-ray flash or TGF – lasting just a few milliseconds but packing a 20-million-volt punch.

"But don't airplanes have lightning rods?" Nick asked. He'd been servicing the light planes at the Flying Club in Alex's absence and had learned about their basic structure.

"Guess they don't work with dark lightning," Michael said ruefully. The origin of dark or dry lightning was still a mystery because it occurred even when there wasn't a cloud in the sky. The American NOAA – the National Oceanic and Atmospheric Administration – confirmed the existence of dark lightning and cited it as the cause of many forest fires. Although many people were still not convinced of its existence, the military tribunal was, and Alex was given a military funeral with full honours.

Michael took Alex's death particularly hard. First his grandfather, then his father, and now his brother – all killed by lightning.

And all firstborns. Amelia was also a firstborn and was turning eighteen in a few months. Hard to believe that funny little girl had grown up to be an independent young woman. But was she at risk? And how the hell could he possibly protect her from lightning, especially when it came out of a clear blue sky? He pushed the thought to the back of his brain and tuned into the conversation again.

"I think we have a pretty good agreement here," Scott said in his lawyer's voice, brightening the mood. "We can lower the price a wee bit in consideration of the large cash down payment, which means we don't have to finance a big chunk of the price. So, call it the family rate."

Scott named a very reasonable price, and Nick gave a low whistle. He'd been saving money for the past five years by banking the bump in pay he got for being McKenzie's manager. A big down payment made the mortgage on the garage affordable.

"Suits me just fine," he said with a smile, sticking out his hand. They all shook on the deal and then went back to work. Nick had a garage to run, Michael had a heifer due to calve, and Scott was meeting with Danny Siggelow, who was back home after being invalided out of the army.

Siggy was injured during a *Blitzkrieg* – a coordinated series of lightning strikes by the Germans throughout Europe. Siggy was stationed in Greece and lost his left leg below the knee in the battle for Crete in April of 1941. He spent several months undergoing treatment in a series of field hospitals and was then repatriated not to Moose Jaw but to Moncton, his place of birth. Alice tried for several months to get him put on a train heading west, but the red tape and regulations were almost insurmountable, especially during wartime. Finally, reason prevailed, and Siggy came home in May of 1943. He spent a few weeks at Ross School, which had been turned into a hospital until the end of the war. Siggy finally came home to Alice and AJ on the first of June. He was unable to return to his job with the railway, so he'd asked Scott for some legal advice on settlements he was being offered. When Scott arrived, Siggy hobbled to the door to greet him with a crutch under his left arm.

"Thanks for coming out to see me," Siggy said. "I could have come into town…"

"I was out this way anyway to see some other folks, so it's no trouble," Scott said. "Does it hurt?"

"Only when I laugh," Siggy chuckled. "Naw, it's OK. Just pisses me off. I shoulda been paying better attention."

"That's a dark sense of humour."

"You know what they say – when you're goin' through hell, keep goin'."

Siggy had spread some documents out on the coffee table and explained each one to Scott.

"This here's the offer from the railway for a partial pension because of disability. And this one's the army insurance form that gives me a veteran's pension. But neither one looks like it's enough to live on, does it? I mean for my whole family." As if on cue, AJ came tumbling into the room and threw himself onto the couch beside his dad.

"I need help with these laces," he said, pointing to his scuffed-up brown shoes, both of which had tangled knots where the laces should be.

"I'm busy now, bub," Siggy said gently. "And anyway, a six-year-old boy should be able to tie his own shoelaces." He was finding it hard to get the right tone with the kid. When Siggy went to war, AJ was a toddler. Now he was a regular boy, although sometimes he still acted like a toddler. After the regimentation of the army, Siggy found the chaos of home life hard to take. It didn't help that he couldn't chase after AJ or play ball with him like a normal dad.

"I don't mind," said Scott. "May I? My daughter, Molly, is about AJ's age and has exactly the same problems. I'm getting good at unsnarling knots."

AJ sat on the floor in front of them and stuck his feet out toward Scott.

"See it's just a matter of following the thread," Scott said. "You do it on that one, and I'll do it on this one. See?" And he showed AJ how to push the aglet back through the tangle of knots until he was left with a crinkled but unknotted shoelace.

"Thanks, Scott," Siggy said.

"Yeah, thanks, Scott," AJ said, leaving the room after tying his shoes.

"Mr. McKenzie to you, bub," Siggy said.

"Scott's fine," Scott said.

"Sorry. I was away a long time, so the boundaries are still a bit unclear."

"No problem, Siggy. He's obviously pretty happy you're home, and he's comfortable around you and other people. That's great. Now let's get back to these pensions. What if you got the money all at once?" Scott asked.

"All at once. How would that work? Is that even possible?"

"We can certainly get a lump sum payment from the railroad. They can amortize it over twenty or thirty years and never miss a penny. The army might be more difficult to deal with, but there are precedents. You could get a payout in the neighbourhood of..." Scott wrote down a figure on the piece of paper. Siggy gasped.

"Really? I've never seen that kind of money in my life. You think I could..."

"I think you could. You don't ask, you don't get, right? So, if you tell me to, we'll ask."

"Yes, please, ask away if you think it's worth it. But what would I do with all that money?"

"Well, you could invest it and live comfortably off the interest," Scott said.

"What, like retire?"

"Why not? You earned it."

"Nah. I don't want to retire. I want to do something. I don't want to just live off the money."

"You could put some away in a college fund for AJ. You could buy some life insurance for Alice and AJ in case you... you know..."

"Yeah. Good idea. But what am *I* gonna do? Like for a job and that? Nobody's hiring cripples."

"You're not a 'cripple' Siggy, whatever that means. What do you want to do? I mean, if you had a chunk of money, how could you use it?"

"You'll think it's weird but..."

"C'mon. Dream a bit. It's your life."

"Well, I'd like to have a bookstore. Quality books, you know?"

"Sounds like a perfect name."

"What?"

"Quality Books. Siggy's Quality Books. The name says it all. Your bookstore. Why not?"

"Yeah, but I don't know the first thing about running a bookstore."

"Ever worked in a store?"

"No, not really. Well, I did work in my uncle's grocery store in Moncton for a couple of summers in high school," Siggy said. "He never paid me. But he taught me how to run the cash register and how to cash out every night. He had a rhyme he always told me: 'Balance the books every night without fail and you'll never have to go to jail.'"

"Words to live by," Scott laughed. "If you like, I can set things in motion, and we'll see where it goes."

Both the railway and the army were happy to draw a line under Siggy's file, and Scott was able to negotiate settlements just over what he had suggested might be possible. He made up a business plan and helped Siggy to lease a storefront a few blocks from his home. There was little overhead because most publishers were happy to supply books on the cuff, expecting payment when they were sold. The only equipment needed was a cash register, an adding machine, and a desk to put them on. Maybe it was his experience in Moncton, but Siggy took to retailing like a natural.

Siggy's Quality Books opened March 1, 1944, in a cozy storefront on Main Street. It was a large space, with room for several easy chairs scattered among the bookshelves, so that customers could sit and read a few pages of a book before deciding to buy it. Most people bought the book.

Chapter 22

There was a boy, a very
strange, enchanted boy –
They say he wandered very
far, over land and sea.
A little shy, but very wise
was he....

Nat Cole's voice was like warm, melted chocolate coming out of the radio. Amelia loved his voice, but loved his piano playing even more, the way he and his trio improvised on standards like *Paper Moon* or the bouncy *Straighten Up and Fly Right*. Just guitar, bass, and piano, but what a sound. No drums, which Amelia appreciated.

"That's Nat 'King' Cole with *Nature Boy*, the number two song on Your Hit Parade for the third week of October, 1948. You're listening to CHAB Moose Jaw, 800 on your dial, and we'll hear the number one song on Your Hit Parade, right after these messages. This is Frank Wallace speaking."

There were several ads for household cleansers, breakfast cereal, and even one for radios. "Twenty-seven all-new De Forest models to choose from!" the announcer proclaimed. Then Doris Day started singing the number one hit, *It's Magic* and Amelia tuned out. She wished they'd play more music like *Twelfth Street Rag* by Pee Wee Hunt. It was number 18 on the Hit Parade, but they only played the Top Ten on the radio. So boring!

Amelia turned her attention to the tomatoes she was growing. More than two-thirds of Saskatchewan was cropland and yet hardly anyone grew fresh vegetables. There was usually a glut of cheap tomatoes and other produce from the market gardens in late summer, but they were costly and scarce the rest of the year. After studying agriculture at the University of Saskatchewan for two years, Amelia returned to work with her parents at Home Farm. She insulated a small machine shed the first summer she was back and built a dozen raised beds which she filled with good soil. She planted tomato seeds and nurtured them with mineral-rich Saskatchewan water, while overhead a series of incandescent filament lamps provided violet-blue light and warmth to help the plants grow from seedlings to sturdy plants heavy with ripening tomatoes. The first crop was planted in August of 1948 and harvested in November. She planted another small crop in September, overlapping crops so that she could produce a steady supply of tomatoes. There was a hungry market for fresh tomatoes, especially during the winter, and she was able to charge an affordable price that easily paid for the cost of production.

"You might think about scaling up this operation a little," Michael said. "We got the big machine shed that's empty except for that old John Deere. Maybe you could use that space?"

"Thanks, Dad, but that's too big for what I want to do."

"But think what you could do with a purpose-built structure. You could cultivate acres of tomatoes in the middle of winter, enough to supply Regina and Saskatoon."

"If this operation were any bigger than what I have now, I wouldn't have a life. Part of the attraction is that it's small. It's just me. You may have noticed I don't play well with others. Never have. So here, I can listen to the radio, do my work, and not have to talk to anyone. If only I could get a phonograph in here, I could listen to Billie Holiday or Charlie Parker. Then I might never leave my little vegetable patch."

"You sound like me a dozen years ago when your Uncle Scott helped us out of a financial jam. But you put into words what I could never get him to understand. That it's about the quality, the satisfaction from making a good product, whatever it is. If it's worth something, people will pay for it. You understand that without going full speed commercial. That's why you're my favourite daughter." He looked at her with that sad-happy look he got when he expressed his emotions. Usually, he just kept quiet and went about his business, talking his problems out with the livestock.

"I'm also your only daughter, Daddy-o, now give me a hand with those bales of peat moss. They're light but awkward, and I want to fork some into all the beds and mix it with the soil before I replant."

While it was perpetual spring inside Amelia's hothouse operation, the world outside was covered in ice. There had been a few warm days at the beginning of February, enough to melt some of the snow that was piling up from a winter that was wetter than usual. Then a cold and nasty wind out of the southeast blew freezing rain across southern Saskatchewan, coating everything in a glaze of ice. Now more snow was needed to cover up the ice and allow for at least a little bit of traction. The sky was gray and low, but the snow that was forecast on the radio had yet to appear.

Despite the conditions, Amelia had to drive into town with a load of tomatoes. Well, she didn't *have* to, but three different stores were expecting a couple of crates each, and the money would help pay for the next crop. So, with Michael's help, she filled half a dozen crates with firm red Beefsteak tomatoes and loaded them into the cab of the Fargo pickup because they'd freeze in the back bed. The old truck was getting on in years, but it had an 84-horsepower six-cylinder engine and a set of 16-inch snow tires on it that could take her almost anywhere. It also had a damned fine heater, so the tomatoes beside her in the cab were toasty warm.

"I'll come with you, Amy," Michael said. "The roads are terrible and..."

"I'll be OK, Dad. It's just winter." And with that, Amelia climbed into the cab and piloted the pickup down the driveway and on into town. The roads were as bad as she expected – icy, rutted, and potholed – so she kept the truck in second gear most of the way. She liked being on her own, able to let thoughts roll through her mind without having to make conversation with someone. She wasn't anti-social. She just wasn't pro-social.

"Morning, Sam," she chirped to the tall produce manager at Butler's Grocery.

"Didn't think I'd see you today. How're the roads?"

"D'you remember how bad they were in early November?" It had been the same combination of a thaw and freezing rain that draped everything in ice.

"That bad?"

"Worse. I'd have better traction on the curling rink," she laughed. "Two cases OK?"

"I'll take more if ya got 'em," Sam said. "People love fresh tamaters in the winter."

"I'll have more ready by the end of the week, so I'll see ya Friday."

"You bet."

When she finished her deliveries, Amelia stopped at Siggy's to pick up a book she'd ordered.

Siggy was born to be a bookseller. He read constantly, loved to talk about books and was always ready to put in special orders, no matter how obscure or expensive the title. The store was thriving. People drove in from miles around to pick up the latest books or magazines and have a bit of a yak and a cup of Siggy's excellent coffee. He bought lightly roasted Brazilian beans that were shipped in from Regina and ground them himself every time he made a fresh pot.

"Is it in?" she asked as she came into the bookstore along with a cold gust of fresh air.

"Just this morning," Siggy said.

"And...?"

"I read the first twenty pages, and oh my, but it's good. The subject material is so fresh and raw, it reads like reportage." Siggy picked up a copy from a pile and handed it to Amelia.

Norman Mailer's *The Naked and the Dead* was about a group of Marines fighting on a Japanese-held island in the Pacific during World War Two and was so popular Siggy couldn't keep it in stock.

Thanks. How much?"

"Four bucks. Expensive, but worth it. Now are you interested in a kind of futuristic book?"

"Like science fantasy?"

"Not really. It's more... well, let's call it a fictionalized commentary about society, if that makes any sense. It's called *1984*, by a British guy called Orwell."

"Not 1948, but *1984*? Hmmm... Well, if you recommend it, then I'll buy it," Amelia said. "As long as people keep buying my tomatoes!"

"Now that's what I call a sensible economy," Siggy laughed.

The old Fargo grumbled about being started up again, and Amelia waited a few minutes for it to warm up enough to drive. Towering eddies of snowflakes waltzed down the middle of the empty street, playing hide and seek with buildings, trees, and telephone poles. It was almost dark, and the town was deserted as the north wind drowned out most other sounds. But Amelia thought she heard a sort of rhythmic singsong coming from somewhere, so she cranked down the window and looked around. Out of the whirling snow, a small, dark man appeared leading a stout horse pulling a cart. As they came up beside the pickup, the man turned his green eyes on Amelia and repeated his song.

"Spare the rod and share the blame. Watch the world go up in flames. Your protection or your shame. Take the rod and fire's tamed."

The man continued leading his horse-drawn cart into the gathering snow, and the little song grew fainter as they faded from view. Amelia shook off a shiver that wanted to run down her spine, turned on the headlights, put the truck in gear, and started the drive home.

The shimmering air was aurora blue and turned even colder. Frost crystals solidified into tiny pellets of hail that pinged on the Fargo's tin hide and rattled on the windshield. Then the hail softened and turned to fluffy snow that floated around the truck like down from a burst pillow. Within minutes, the snow was packed into the ruts, muting the tires and making the ride smoother. Amelia could only see a few feet in front of her, so she kept the truck in second gear and crawled along.

She was almost home when blue-white lightning prismed the snowflakes and dazzled her eyes as it sparkled down the road toward her. Amelia stood on the brake, and the heavy old Fargo rumbled to a stop. Lightning vibrated all around her now, the elemental power playing over the truck and crackling along contours, emitting a high, delirious hum that faded as it passed over her and continued down the road.

Amelia sat for a moment with a high-pitched whine singing in her ears as she tried to get her bearings. Slowly, the throaty rumble of the Fargo's engine became the dominant note, the shimmering air faded, and fat flakes of snow continued to fall. Amelia put the truck in gear and plowed her way down the road and home.

"What the hell happened to you?" Jenny asked when Amelia came through the front door. "You look like you were rode hard and put up wet. C'mere, let me help you out of that wet coat and get you something warm and dry to put on."

Amelia caught a glimpse of herself in the hall mirror and shuddered. Her hair looked wild, her eyes stared, and her skin appeared sallow.

"Storm," she managed to say. "Lightning." She shed her coat, shivered, and shrugged into a thick Arran shawl that her mother wrapped around her and warmed her like a hug.

"Lightning? In the winter?" Jenny recalled Michael talking about seeing winter lightning when he was a kid. Something about a horse getting spooked.

"I swear, I saw it," Amelia said. "And the wire parts of the empty tomato crates are fused and black."

"Michael!" Jenny hollered. "You here?" A moment later, Michael came up from the basement.

"Just working on that latch thingy for your crates, Amy," he said, brushing sawdust off his calloused hands. "Hey, what the hell happened to you, honey?"

"Didn't you tell me you saw lightning in the winter one time?" Jenny asked him. "When you were young?"

"Thundersnow," Michael said, with a low whistle.

"That's it," Jenny said. "Thundersnow. Did you get hit by lightning, Amy? Thundersnow? My poor darling!"

"I think so. The Fargo was vibrating. And there was a blue light that kind of washed over the truck."

"Them tires," Michael said. "Glad I put them tires on there."

"What tires? How'd we get from lightning to tires?"

"See, them tires are sixteen-inchers. Lots of rubber. Good grounding. Otherwise..." Michael looked away for a moment, not wanting to think what otherwise could mean. "But you're OK?"

"Well, other than the ringing in my ears and looking like a crazy person, yeah I'm OK."

"Well, I suppose you might be allowed to look a fright if you survived being hit by lightning," Jenny said, pulling her daughter closer.

"Is it the Curse?" Amelia asked. "You know, like Grampa and... and his father?"

"There is no 'curse,' dear child. Just a lot of superstitions and malarkey. Now let's get you a cup of tea and a hot bath."

Chapter 23

The front door of Siggy's Quality Books was open to the gentle May breezes and the sound of a student marching band tootling past along Main Street, part of the Kinsmen International Competition. They were playing *City of Harmony*, and the familiar words came unbidden to Siggy's head.

Moose Jaw, Moose Jaw, City of Harmony. Right in step with the musical jamboree...

It was 1953 and optimism was in fashion. People were buying cars and houses and having lots of children who filled the schools and needed clothes and sports equipment and books and pets and bicycles. And food. And then more clothes as they grew older. It was a workable model, and the economy was humming along rather nicely.

Friendliest town for miles around. It's all happening here. This is the place setting the pace. Any time of the year...

The cheery song was at odds with the box of new books Siggy was unpacking. Copies of Ray Bradbury's *Fahrenheit 451* were selling as fast as he could get them in. Although it was set in a grim future, the burning of books reminded him of the very recent past. A yellowing twenty-year-old clipping from the *Moncton Daily Times* was framed and hung near the cash register to remind himself and anyone else who cared, what can happen while you're not looking.

BLACKLISTED BOOKS TO BE BURNED IN GERMANY
Preparations for Huge Bonfires Tonight – Nazi Official To Speak

Berlin – May 10 1933 (AP) – Blacklisted books from private
as well as public libraries were piled high today on
"Kultur's altars" throughout Germany for burning tonight.
Schoolboys enthusiastically rushed final preparations for
the huge bonfires. Nazi student committees of action have
been working at top speed for more than a week arranging
for the purging of the libraries of "unGerman influences."

The banality of evil cheerfully reported by the Associated Press scared Siggy just as much now as it did back then. He was 26 years old in 1933 and still bouncing from job to job. Every morning, he went to the Moncton Public Library and scanned the newspaper want ads for job listings along with the rest of the unemployed men, then he walked for miles following up leads that led to nothing but sore feet. In the afternoon, he returned to the library and read books for a couple of hours. He was undiscriminating and omnivorous, resulting in a sort of scattergun education.

"Hey, Siggy. You got the Bradbury in yet?" Amelia McKenzie asked as she came breezing into the store with baby Zach on her hip, bringing with them a waft of fresh spring air.

"Blah, blah," said Zach.

"Yes, ma'am. Right here," Siggy said, brandishing the red, black, and white cover of *Fahrenheit 451*. "I've only read the first fifty pages so far, but it's a little too close to the truth. Surprised it hasn't been banned."

"Well, the Irish just banned Huxley's *Point Counter Point* and most of Steinbeck's work, so maybe it's just a matter of time," Amelia said. "Can't have people reading about book burning, sex, or immorality, doncha know?"

"We live in a dangerous time, and I fear it will only get worse for kids like Zach. 'Orwellian,' some might say. Is that too pessimistic?"

"Ever since you got me reading Orwell five years ago, I see dystopia and Big Brother everywhere!" Amelia laughed. "But then you read about what Joe McCarthy's doing in the states with the House Un-American Activities Committee. They don't like anybody who doesn't think like they do, which is pretty much everyone. Say anything against them, and you're tied up in legal knots for years. Who elects these politicians?"

"It's scary to think that half the people out there are below average intelligence," Siggy chuckled.

"Maybe intelligent people just tell themselves better lies," Amelia said. Before the discussion could get too morose, Zach let out a shriek of joy, his contribution to the conversation.

"He's really getting big," Siggy said.

"Yeah, he's a chunk alright," Amelia said. "Eats like a farmhand, too. Kid can really put away the groceries." She shifted her hip and hiked the six-month-old boy into a more comfortable position. "You get Alice to give me a telephone call, and we'll set up a visit, OK? I gotta go pick up Allie."

"Sure, thing Amy," Siggy said. "Hi to Jamie."

Amelia McKenzie and Jamie Sinclair had met four years earlier when she was working at the Coop as a cashier. Jamie had taken over the family farm south of town a few years before when his father died unexpectedly. His mother had spent most of her days in the living room, staring out the window, so Jamie cared for her, grew wheat and barley like his father had, and came to town once a week to shop for groceries. He always went to Amelia's checkout, even if the lineup was longer. After the third time, and because he was so obvious, Amy asked him straight out.

"Are you in love with me?"

"I might just be," Jamie said without missing a beat. "The way you run that cash register and all, I just might be."

"You're cheeky too," she said, grinning while she rang in his groceries. "I don't mind cheek." She also didn't mind that Jamie was well-built, a hard worker with an open face, a ready smile, and blue eyes that got bluer if he was smiling.

"That'll be eighteen sixty-four," she said as the cash door dinged open.

"I don't have any cash, so can I write you a cheque? We got an account here. Sinclair?" He bent over the counter and wrote out the cheque.

"You're Jamie Sinclair?"

"Uh, yeah...."

"Heard you were a good ballplayer," Amelia said.

"I play some. I know your first name is Amy 'cause it's on your tag right there," he said, pointing to her lapel. "But what's your last name, seein's how you know mine?"

"I'm Amelia McKenzie. My father Michael farms just north of town."

"I know your dad," Jamie said. "He comes to the Wheat Producers meetings. He's a smart man and a damn good farmer. Look I hate to hold up the line, so maybe we could meet some other place besides this store. Whaddya say we grab a burger at the Melon Dew sometime?"

"We both like my dad, and we both like baseball, so I guess we'll get along OK. How 'bout tonight? I gotta eat, and I finish at seven. Is that too late for you?"

"That'd be about right. Get these groceries home and see to mom, then come back in and pick you up. Sound good?"

"You bet."

Jamie coached and played second base for the Moose Jaw Canucks of the Southern Baseball League, which also included the Delisle Commodores, the Notre Dame Hounds, the Estevan Maple Leafs, and the Swift Current Indians. It was a competitive league made up of young men who all dreamed of being called up to The Show any day now. The pitches were hard, the play was fast, rivalries were intense, and teams attracted hundreds of vocal followers on hot summer nights. But like anything else in Saskatchewan, baseball was at the mercy of the weather gods. Games were rained out, hailed out, and called because it was just too damned hot to play, or because the bugs were too bad. One game was called on account of rain *and* dust, a kind of mud storm.

When team manager Bud Riley heard that Jamie and Amelia were going to be married, he made Jamie a proposition.

"Whaddya say we hold the wedding at Ross Wells?"

"We?" Jamie asked. Already it was 'the' wedding, not his and Amelia's wedding.

"C'mon, it'll be a grand way to celebrate our new ballpark. You could get hitched at home plate. I know an umpire, Father Francis from Notre Dame. We could ask him to... whaddya call it?"

Bud Riley was unfamiliar with weddings, marriage, or anything else to do with the whole relationship thing. His only relationship was with baseball. He managed the Canucks through the spring and summer season then spent the winter on the phone horse-trading players for next year's team. He had no time for anything else.

"*Officiate*, Bud. I think that's the word you're looking for. You want an umpire to officiate at my wedding?"

"Yeah, that's it. He's a father. I mean a priest. You're Catholic, right?"

"Baseball fans don't wanna pay to see me and Amelia get married, Bud," Jamie said patiently. "I'm not a marquee player like Curly." Curly Bradshaw was the Canucks' star first baseman who could hit, run, and field better than anyone. Once, he was called in to pitch when the bullpen was depleted and struck out three batters in a row with only a dozen pitches. "They wanna see us play baseball and beat the pants off of Estevan, which may be a tougher team than we think. They're stacked with ringers from the states – Minnesota, even Arizona, where they play baseball all year long."

"But Curly ain't getting' married, Jamie. You are," Bud said. "Think about it anyway. It'll be great, you'll see. Nice summer day. Ballpark. True love. People eat that stuff up with a spoon. It'll be packed."

"And then I'm s'posed to play baseball after I get married in front of hundreds of people?" Jamie didn't like where this was going. If the Canucks lost, his wedding day would forever be associated with a bad memory. "I don't think so, Bud. I know Amelia doesn't want to get married in front of a bunch of strangers."

"They're not strangers, Jamie, they're your fans."

"Dollars to donuts Amelia won't go for it," Jamie said. "And if she says no, I say no."

But Amelia wasn't entirely opposed to the idea.

"It's a swell way to mark the ballpark's inaugural year," she said when he told her about Bud's idea. "Think of it as a way to do something for Moose Jaw, to make a memory for a whole bunch of people, and also get married and play some ball. What's not to like?"

"I don't want our marriage to be a spectacle," Jamie said. "It's about you and me, not baseball."

"You're such a rank sentimentalist, Jamie Sinclair, and I love you for it. But we won't let it become a spectacle. We'll have a five-minute ceremony at home plate, just as quick as it would be at the courthouse, and then you'll play ball. People will forget all about us as soon as the first pitch is thrown."

"You make it sound easy."

"It's just gettin' married. The hard stuff is still ahead of us."

The day was flawless. The temperature was in the low 80s. Not a cloud marred the cornflower blue sky, and a light southerly breeze kept the bugs away. As the fans filed through the gates, they passed a small, dark man standing beside the entrance with a horse and cart and a sign that read:

THORSON LIGHTNING RODS

He repeated a little song as his green eyes scanned each one of them as they walked by.

"Spare the rod and share the blame. Watch the world go up in flames. Your protection or your shame. Take the rod and fire's tamed."

Most people didn't give him a second look or forgot about him as soon as they were inside the ballpark, which was gussied up with bunting and banners. The summer smell of hot dogs, fried onions, and popcorn wafted through the air and the seats filled up quickly. Jamie's mom was ensconced right behind home plate, along with Jenny and Michael McKenzie.

At precisely five minutes to seven, Mendelssohn's Wedding March crackled out of the bleacher speakers as Amelia and Jamie walked onto the field. The bride wore blue jeans and a crisp white shirt. The groom wore number 24 for the Moose Jaw Purity Canucks. Fr. Francis had argued for a longer ceremony, but Amelia made the case for a shorter one by appealing to the priest's love of baseball.

"The fans are there for the game. They won't like it, and may get restless if they have to wait too long," she told Fr Francis. Amelia made sure the service wasn't larded by a bunch of religious mumbo jumbo by writing the vows herself, which the good father dutifully, if regretfully, read.

"Do you, Amelia McKenzie, take Jamie Sinclair for your husband?" asked Fr Francis.

"I do," Amelia said.

"And do you, Jamie Sinclair, take Amelia McKenzie for your wife?"

"I do."

"I now pronounce you husband and wife. God bless you both."

The crowd cheered and whooped as Fr Francis slipped out of his priestly robe to reveal his umpire uniform. He put on his mask, turned to face the mound, and hollered: "Play ball!"

His words were still echoing across the infield when the clear summer sky was split by a crackling bolt of lightning that decapitated a tree on the other side of the right field fence. After a moment's stunned silence and realizing that no one was hurt, the crowd got to their feet and roared their approval, hooting and clapping like they'd survived Armageddon or seen the greatest show on earth.

"I'm gonna make me a bat outta that tree," Curly Bradshaw was heard to say.

The Moose Jaw Canucks went on to beat the Estevan Maple Leafs 11 – 3, including two grand slams by Marrillo and Sinclair. Verlane Dupray had a devilish smile on her 73-year-old face as she joined the rest of the happy fans making their way out of the ballpark after the game.

Chapter 24

Pope Pius was in grave condition after suffering a stroke, the Russians beat the Americans in the space race by launching Sputnik, and the Yankees beat the Braves 6-2 to win the 1958 World Series. Scott McKenzie felt that a more important story deserved a spot on the front page, too, but it was buried deep in the business pages under a tepid headline:

STEADY FARM INCOME PLEDGED

PC Resolution Also Calls · for Price Stabilization for wheat producers

As the MP for Moose Jaw, he had sponsored the resolution in the House, but there was no mention of his name in the article. He lamented how petty he'd become after ten years in Ottawa, but that was the bread and butter of the business. Name recognition. See and be seen. Talk to everyone and make sure they know your name. It was all self-promotion. He remembered what John Gordon Ross had said all those years ago, when he encouraged Scott to run for city council. "It's surprising how much you can get accomplished if you don't get too attached to the results."

Hard to believe it was more than thirty years ago, before the war, even before the Depression.

Scott had already told the party that he would not be running in the 1962 election, but he would serve out his term. In Ottawa, he was the point man for the government when reporters wanted a quote on farm policy, which wasn't often. Back in the riding, he had to do one or two interviews a day, which he saw as a necessary evil, part of his job. Most reporters were more concerned with headlines or quotable clips than with the boring details of trade agreements and stabilization measures. A rare exception was Frank Wallace at CHAB, the Moose Jaw radio station, and an affiliate of the CBC. Franklin Wallace was unlike most reporters in that he had a degree in Agriculture and seemed to know what he was talking about. He asked intelligent questions and then waited for McKenzie to finish his answer before asking another question.

The two of them had an agreeable and informative twenty-minute chat while hundreds of farmers listened live across the province as they ate their midday meal. After the program, Wallace and McKenzie were shaking hands when there was a mighty boom and a loud metallic clanging right above them, as if someone had dropped a grand piano from a great height. Plaster drifted down from the ceiling like fine snow as they rushed to the window to see a crowd of people gathering down below on Main Street.

"Was it an earthquake?" McKenzie asked.

"In Saskatchewan?" Wallace asked. "Not likely. Something bad though. Let's see if the stairs are intact and get outside."

On the street, people pointed and stared at the top corner of the five-story building in which CHAB had its studios. The walls were peeled away to reveal an empty office complete with a desk and a small table, like a student's diorama. Smoke plumed from the roof so Scott ran back into the building to call the fire department from the pay phone in the lobby. The fire hall was just around the corner and in a few minutes a crew extended the ladder on the truck to get a better look at the damage.

"Looks like a lightning strike on your radio tower," said Capt. Merv Atkinson as he came back down the ladder while powerful hoses played on the tumbled, smoldering bricks.

"But we have lightning rods on two corners, precisely to keep the tower from getting hit."

"Well, they're OK, but the roof got hit ennaway," Atkinson shrugged. "So, maybe the lightning come down between them two rods. We'll know more when we get 'er cooled down, and then we can get up there for a looksee."

I am a being of Heaven and Earth, of thunder and lightning, of rain and wind, of the galaxies. - Eden Ahbez

Chapter 25

"That looks like frostbite," Dr. Kulcheski said. "You been working with dry ice or something, AJ?" AJ Siggelow's fingertips were scorched and blackened, and the hair was singed off his arms up to his elbows.

"No, sir, I was working on my car," AJ Siggelow replied. "I like to keep her tuned up, so I was rebuilding the carburetor when... well, it's hard to describe... kinda like a shock except..." He paused and tried to find words to explain what had happened that morning.

He'd been under the hood of the big Merc, removing the carburetor and laying each piece carefully onto a leather mat laid across the broad fender. The car's sleek oxblood body was in showroom condition, and the chassis and drive train were as solid as when the car left the assembly line fourteen years ago. He liked to keep ahead of the car's maintenance, and so he was borrowing his folks' garage for a few days to rebuild the carburetor.

He was reaching for a set of calipers when a sizzling flash of light spiked down from the ceiling of the garage and connected with the car's engine. AJ was able to leap back out of the way, bonking his head on the upraised hood as he did. His fingertips were smoking and blackened and hurt like hell as he looked up to see if the overhead light had short-circuited or if a squirrel or a cat had messed with the wiring. There was a hole in the garage roof the size of an easy chair and nothing but blue sky above it. As AJ turned to go outside and have a look at the damage and seek medical attention for his fingers, a young woman came running into the garage. She was slim, with tousled sandy hair and brilliant blue eyes.

"You OK? What happened?" she asked. "Oh, your poor fingers. Let's get you to a doctor. Can you walk?"

"Yeah, I guess so. I'm AJ, and my doctor's just around the corner on Main Street."

"I'm Molly," she said as she took his elbow and steered him down Hochelaga to Main.

Dr. Kulcheski's waiting room was full, but when the nurse saw AJ's hands, she moved him to the head of the line.

"Sounds like lightning to me, AJ," said Dr. Kulcheski a few minutes later. "Come through your roof, you say?"

"Just about blew it off," AJ said.

"Did you see it, miss?"

"No, Doc, I just heard the crash and came running." Molly McKenzie had been happily painting in her studio when all hell broke loose next door.

"Lucky it didn't catch on fire," AJ said. "But, doc, how can there be lightning when there wasn't a cloud in the sky?"

"They call it positive lightning. I read about it in the *National Geographic*."

"What's... ?"

"Positive lightning? Coulda been from a storm miles away," Dr. Kulcheski explained as he bandaged AJ's blasted fingertips. "Crazy stuff travels through the sky horizontally, then takes a notion to go to ground."

"Why me? Why not a power pole or a radio tower? They're higher and closer to the damn sky."

"Or why not my studio next door?" Molly asked. "Why his garage?"

"Now you're asking me something I don't know. Maybe that hunk of iron you were working on looked attractive to this wandering lightning bolt."

"My Merc? But it was in a garage. Under the roof. I don't get it."

"Oh, you got it OK. Heh heh. Sorry, but you're lucky that garage roof took most of the

hit, otherwise you mighta got blasted worse."
The doctor finished his work, washed his
hands, and turned back to AJ. "You're one
lucky fella, AJ. You leave those bandages on
for a few days, now, you hear? Then use that
salve I gave you, and you'll be back tinkering
with that engine before you know it. Come
see me if you have any trouble."

"I can walk home with you if you want,"
Molly said. "My studio's right next door to
your garage."

"Thanks for coming to my rescue." They
turned off Main and walked back up
Hochelaga.

"That was your car in the garage? That
beautiful maroon Merc?"

"Oxblood, not maroon, but yes, ma'am,"
AJ said. "Forty-nine Mercury, 245 cubic
inch eight-cylinder powerhouse develops..."

"...a hundred and ten horsepower, yeah.
What a beast. You fix 'em?"

"Yes, ma'am, I do." AJ didn't know
where all this ma'am stuff was coming from
but he'd never met a woman who cared much
for cars unless she was getting a ride in one.
This was all new territory.

"So, you live there?"

"My folks do. My dad runs Siggy's Books
on Main."

"I love that bookstore," Molly said. "My
father is Scott McKenzie, his law office is
over on Langdon Crescent. But enough
about our fathers. How are you doing?"

"Yeah, I'm OK, thanks. Hurts a bit. Those painkillers the doc gave me help, though."

"You are *so* lucky, AJ. You must have horseshoes stashed somewhere because this is your lucky day."

"Getting hit by lightning is lucky?"

"Surviving it is. My grandfather, my great grandfather, and my Uncle Alex were all killed by lightning."

"Jesus, I'm so sorry. I didn't... I mean, that's tough. Are you afraid of it? Lightning, I mean?"

"Well, people talk about the McKenzie Curse, but I don't believe in any of that stuff. Although it is kinda spooky, isn't it?"

"Very spooky. Am I in danger, being around you?"

"Hah! Naw, like I said, this was your lucky day. Not only did you get hit by lightning and live to tell the tale, but you also met me. And this is me." She pointed at the Siggelow house with the hole in the garage roof, then moved her finger toward a tidy little bungalow and behind that bungalow was a tidy little laneway house with windows on the north and east sides.

"C'mon in," Molly said. "If your fingers aren't too sore." AJ followed her inside.

The main room was larger than it appeared from the outside. Stretched blank canvasses were stacked against one wall, treated, and left to dry. A large easel was set up to take the best advantage of the steady northern light. There was a little kitchen in one corner and a curtained-off bedroom at the back. AJ breathed in the heady essence of oil paints, turpentine, wood, and canvas.

"You live here?" AJ asked.

"Sometimes. When I'm working on a painting. My grandma Janet owned the house out front and let me build this place a few years ago. But she died last year, so now I rent it from the new owners. Otherwise, I live at my folks' place up the hill. But when I'm here, I sometimes hear you revving the Merc next door," Molly said.

"Sorry. That's probably when I'm tuning it up. I have to rev it sometimes to make sure it's firing properly. Does it bother you?"

"Are you kidding? That throb is the soundtrack for my paintings!"

AJ breathed in the heady essence of oil paints, turpentine, wood, and canvas, but could make no sense of the work on the easel. It was a large canvas with a warring hodgepodge of clashing colours crisscrossing each other in angry slashes.

"Yeah, I don't understand it either," Molly laughed at AJ's puzzled expression. "I just kinda go berserk with paint, and people pay me ridiculous amounts of money for the result."

"Are you famous?" AJ didn't know the names of any artists and wouldn't have recognized any of their work anyway. He was treading on thin ice here and thought he'd better retreat before he screwed up everything with this beautiful woman.

"Ha ha. No, I'm not famous. But you'll see my work in the Esso building in Calgary, the Winnipeg Stock Exchange, and a few other places, where they like big, bold paintings for their lobbies or boardrooms."

"I had no idea..."

"Hey, don't tell anyone. Between you and me, it's a bit of a scam, but if they wanna pay..."

"That's an interesting way to make a living. I thought all artists were starving in garrets or something."

"Only the unimaginative ones, or the ones that feel that selling their art to a wealthy corporation would be selling out their artistic souls. What a riot!"

"Do you?"

"Sell my soul? Nah. It's still around here somewhere. It's just a simple equation. They have money and want art, and I make art and want money. You remember what Willie Sutton said?"

"Who's Willie Sutton?"

"Bank robber. Cops asked him why he kept robbing banks. He said, 'cuz that's where the money is. Corporations are where the money is, so I sell them my art."

"You wanna go for a ride sometime?" AJ was thinking he could listen to Molly talk forever, especially if they were cruising along Highway 20 through the Qu'Appelle Valley or taking a drive down to Assiniboia with the windows rolled down.

"In your Merc? Damn right I do," Molly said. "When? Now?"

"Oh, anytime. I just have to put that carburetor back together."

"With those hands?"

"Oh yeah." AJ looked at his bandaged hands and sighed.

"Could I help?" Molly held up her hands with the fingers splayed. "Ten digits, and they're all yours if you tell me what to do."

"I don't want you to ruin your hands."

"Look at these mitts. Turpentine, water, oil paints, gesso, Xacto knives – they're used to rough treatment. So, the sooner we get that carburetor back together, the sooner we can hit the road. But you should lie down first. You've had quite a day."

"Yeah, I should go," AJ said.

"No, you can lay down right here." Molly led him to the bedroom at the back and helped him to lie down on the double bed. Then she lay down beside him.

"This might not be a good idea," AJ said, thinking it was a helluva good idea and he should just shut up.

"Don't you worry. Just lay back and relax."

"But I don't... I haven't got..."

"... a condom? No worries, AJ. Margaret Sanger took care of all that."

"Who's Margaret... ?"

"...Sanger. The founder of the American Birth Control League? You know, we've had birth control pills for a couple of years now, right? This is 1963. You do read the papers?"

"No, I..." The subject really hadn't come up. AJ had a few friends who were girls, but they didn't talk about stuff like this. He'd never had a steady girlfriend so all this was new. And AJ did read the newspapers – well, the sports pages and the comics on the weekend anyway.

"Well, let's not spend our time talking about Margaret Sanger," Molly laughed. "Let's just enjoy each other's company. But protect those hands. Let me do all the work."

Chapter 26

"Looks like a friggin' beer label," Gordie Felske said.

"I kinda like it. Simple. Red and white. Any school kid could draw it," Wilf Franklin opined. Wilf drove the Caron school bus in the early morning and mid-afternoon, but otherwise, he had a lot of time on his hands and liked to spend some of it drinking Siggy's excellent coffee and talking about current events.

"Looks like a school kid did draw it," Gordie said with a laugh. "I always hated drawing the Union Jack in school, though. Had to get out the protractor and the triangle thingy and get all the lines just right or Mrs. Broda would whap you on the back of your hand with her steel-edged ruler."

"But at least the Red Ensign stood for something," said Nick Rizzo. "That red maple leaf banner stands for nothing. It looks like a logo for some company that makes sporting goods or something. There's no heraldry there, no history."

"Well, as far as I'm concerned, the Red Ensign stands for empire and Britain and saying 'mother may I' to the queen every time we want to turn around, so why not have our own flag instead of somebody else's?" Wilf said.

The Canadian Red Ensign had a red background with Britain's red-white-and-blue Union Jack taking up the top left quarter and a shield with provincial coats of arms in the lower right corner. It was based on the ensign flown by British merchant ships since 1707 and had been the de facto Canadian national flag since Confederation.

"Anyway, this is all just a distraction," Nick said. "Don't we have bigger fish to fry, like getting the economy going again? Getting people working again? I already lived through the dirty thirties, thank you very much. I don't need another Depression. We're halfway through the sixties, and so far, I'm not impressed."

Terms like *stagflation* and *recession* were tossed around like economic hand grenades, and theories were thick on the ground, but nobody really seemed to know why the economy was still sluggish and unemployment was so high. Meanwhile, the entire country was consumed with the Great Flag Debate. Should Canada retain the current British Red Ensign as Canada's flag, or fly a new banner for a new country: a red maple leaf on a white background flanked by red panels? The Maple Leaf. Forever.

"Well, it just looks like a beer label," Gordie repeated. "Canadian beer at the sign of the maple leaf, that's our country, eh."

"Beer?" asked AJ as he came into the shop. "Who's drinking beer at 11 o'clock in the morning?"

"It's the flag, son. Everyone's in a tizzy about the new flag," Siggy said, throwing up his hands in mock despair. "What'll we do? What'll we do?"

"It's a serious business, Siggy," said Gordie. "It's how people think of Canada. Do you want them to see us as nothing more than a bloody beer label?"

"I like it," said AJ. "It's simple, and it's ours, not Britain's."

"Spoken like a young man without an understanding of history," Gordie said, not unkindly.

"Well, Pearson's about to argue his case at the Legion in Winnipeg next week," Wilf said.

"They'll eat him for lunch," Nick said. "He's crazy to even try to convince them."

"If he can convince that bunch of monarchists, he can convince anyone," said Wilf. Lester Pearson was the prime minister of a minority Liberal government during an economic slump, and it looked like his political days were numbered. But he seized on the issue of giving the country a new flag as a way to inspire confidence and hope in the Canadian economy. Later that year, he would succeed, and the maple leaf would become Canada's flag.

1964 was also the year that US President Lyndon B. Johnson signed the Civil Rights Act, Saskatchewan's Ross Thatcher became the first Liberal to form a provincial government outside Quebec in a generation, and Northern Dancer became the first Canadian-bred racehorse to win the Kentucky Derby and charge million-dollar stud fees. But most Canadians were still talking about the flag.

In the meantime, AJ needed a book that had nothing to do with horses or flags or politics.

"Sorry to interrupt the discussion, but did you get that book in Dad?"

"I did indeed. Quite the story," Siggy said. *The Man Who Rode the Thunder* was William Rankin's first-person account of bailing out of his fighter jet and plunging 50,000 feet over the space of nine minutes, falling through every type of weather imaginable, including lightning and ear-splitting thunder. Written in 1950, the book was hard to find, but Siggy had eventually tracked a copy down in a used bookstore in Eugene, Oregon.

"How're your hands after that strike, AJ?" Gordie asked.

"Still a bit stiff, Gordie, thanks for asking. But I can set points and fix the wiring or whatever kinda fine work there is, so it's OK." AJ was a good mechanic, self-taught but quick to learn. Nick sometimes hired him for a week now and then to help with a backlog. But people were keeping their money in their pockets, waiting to see if times got better, and even McKenzie Mechanical had to lay off more than a third of its staff over the last few years.

"Don't go scaring yourself with that book now, eh?" Siggy said. "That firstborn stuff is a load of the well-known article."

"Don't worry Dad. What do I owe you?" AJ asked.

"Early birthday present, son," Siggy grinned. AJ's birthday was not until October, but it was a good bet he was broke because he put every extra dime he had into his beloved Merc.

"Thanks. See y'all," AJ said on his way out of the store. "I'll be over later to help with those eavestroughs, Dad."

Siggy and Alice had been living in the same old house since AJ was a baby, and the place needed constant upkeep. Old Bakelite fuses blew, cast-iron plumbing leaked and rusted, porches sagged, and stairs creaked. AJ had been trying for a few years to get his folks to move into a newer, smaller place, and took another shot at it later that day when he went over to clean the eavestroughs.

"You could move to a bungalow that's all on one level, Dad," AJ said from up on the ladder. He was throwing down gobbets of wet leaves onto a pile to be added to the compost later. "Wide doors so you could scoot around in your chair if you wanted to."

"I don't want to move at my age," Siggy said from the porch.

"Gimme a break! You're not even sixty, Dad. You guys would find it so much easier."

"AJ's got a point," Alice said, coming out onto the porch. "A newer place with a good furnace and a heated garage." Right now, their five-year-old Buick was parked in an unheated carport and could be hard to start some winter mornings.

"But this place is so close to the bookshop," Siggy said. "Where are we going to find…"

"…a place even closer? How about right around the corner? It's a thousand square feet, heated garage, back deck, and no stairs."

"This place exists?" Alice was wide-eyed.

"Mom, it's a beaut. Saw it on my walk over here. Sign just went up."

"I don't know. We have so much stuff." Siggy never threw away anything. Books, tools, pieces of wire, orphan lumber, windowpanes, and more books. He kept every can of paint he ever bought in case he might need that colour again, even though most of the contents had hardened beyond use. Back issues of *Time Magazine* took up valuable real estate in the basement next to boxes of more books. He had three ladders and could climb none of them.

"I can help you sort through all that stuff," AJ said. "You might have some valuable merchandise there, Pops. Maybe make a fortune on what's in your basement."

Siggy and Alice moved that spring. The collection of superannuated issues of *Time Magazine* went to a collector in Regina for more money than the cost of the move. Many of the books went to the Moose Jaw Public Library, and the rest were donated to the Sally Ann. The ladders and tools went to a good home on South Hill, and the Buick was happy to move into the heated garage.

Chapter 27

***Demand for Sask CrudeSparks
Intense Search***

The story was buried way back in the newspaper, right before the comics, but Scott McKenzie took note. It was the mid-sixties, and the country was still in the economic doldrums. But the world always wants oil. Against prevailing wisdom, he'd put quite a lot of money into oil stocks when they were sagging over the past several years and had watched the value double, then double again as more of the world became mechanized and needed all sorts of petroleum products from plastics to liquid hydrogen. Increased activity in the Saskatchewan industry meant jobs, investment, and taxes for both the provincial and federal governments.

Scott wondered how long the government could keep its fingers out of the oil patch. He'd heard whispers of a campaign to help pay down the federal deficit by wringing more money out of resource industries by tying them up in complex regulations. This might be a good time to cash in before the industry was regulated out of existence. He was sixty-two and thinking about winding up the law practice and exploring other possibilities. He had stepped down as MP before the last election and just as well. He likely would have been defeated.

Eleanor had been gone for two years, dead at 58 from pancreatic cancer that took her in just two months. He still heard her voice in the house, singing some pop song out of tune and with half the words wrong. He still wanted to find her hair in the sink, her many pairs of shoes cluttering the hall closet, a drawer she'd left open or a lid left unscrewed. All those little things that once irked him now came back to haunt him, and he'd give anything, everything, to have them back. It all went by so fast. Twenty-six years of what was sometimes a tumultuous marriage didn't seem long enough to get it right. They were always too busy living to examine their lives closely. Eleanor was a dynamo, a force of nature. You wanted to be caught up in her weather, hoped that it was her coming through the front door and bringing that breath of springtime optimism no matter what the season.

Molly and AJ had bought a house in the neighbourhood and were expecting their first child. Scott's first grandkid. And Robin was working in the Agriculture faculty at the University of Saskatchewan in Saskatoon.

Maybe it was time for him to focus less on working and more on playing, especially with his grandchildren. Meanwhile, he had a curling game to get to. He played in a recreational doubles league with Avery Sloan, a Crown prosecutor, every Tuesday.

The weather had turned cold, and he was glad of the remote starter for his Lincoln. The seats were toasty warm, and the engine purred as he drove through the snow-packed streets to the curling rink. It was only in the past year that he'd had time to play with any regularity, and he noticed his game had improved markedly. He got to the rink a little early and watched as AJ and his partner Jamie Sinclair played the final end of their game.

"You gotta raise our rock into the eight-foot maybe about yea," AJ hollered from the other end of the rink. He held up his broom with his hands about 18 inches apart on the shaft to indicate to Jamie just how far yea was. AJ wore bright yellow railway gloves so that Jamie could see his signals from a hundred and fifty feet away. They were playing a game of doubles against Ron Kowalchuk and David 'Deadeye' Dunn. Dave's left eye was sightless thanks to an errant branch in the BC forest, where he worked for a gyppo logging outfit near Klemtu back in the late fifties. Even so, he consistently put three or four rocks in the house while his opponents were still putting up guards, hence his nickname. This game had come down to the final end, tied two all.

Jamie learned to curl when he was a teenager, when he'd done some work for Gordie Bradner, who farmed down the road from the Sinclair place. Gordie used to raise turkeys in a long wide Quonset hut next to his barn, but the cost of raising the birds was more than he could sell them for, so he got rid of the last batch one spring, cleared out all the equipment, and left the barn to air out over the summer. About half past September, he called on Jamie for some help.

"Gonna turn that turkey barn into a curling rink," Gordie said in his oh-nothin' way. "Room enough for two sheets, I figure, with a walkway in between. Gimme a hand?"

"Sure," said Jamie. "But how you gonna make ice?" He envisioned some kind of generator running 24/7 to keep a little ice plant humming.

Gordie spread his arms and looked around. "We got five months of solid winter here in Saskatchewan, so who needs an ice plant?" He'd already laid down a metal grid for the ice to adhere to. "What I need help with is flooding the barn to make ice while I still got the water turned on outside. I'm hoping we can do successive floods before we get into the deep freeze weather in November, and I have to turn off the outside water. So, there's a little hurry-up involved. You in?"

Jamie said he was in.

They flooded the gridded floor of the Quonset and let nature take its course. Incremental applications of water every afternoon for a couple of weeks turned into bonded layers of ice. By early October, there was a good base, so Gordie and Jamie painted the lines and the concentric circles of the house at either end of each sheet. When the paint was dry, they flooded the rink several more times until it was frozen solid, but the markings were still visible. Jamie had the job of sprinkling the ice surface with water droplets to give it a pebbled finish. There was still a whiff of ammonia from the turkeys if you breathed in deeply enough, but it wasn't too bad. And the ice was keen and diamond hard. Jamie became one of the rink rats, helping to prep the ice in exchange for enough time to play six ends. That's all anyone ever played. After six, you had to go in before you froze. He missed that brilliant outdoor ice, but he certainly did not miss curling at twenty below.

Jamie and AJ had been doubles partners for three seasons. They were an odd couple because their curling strategies were polar opposites. Jamie was a risk-taker. AJ, a dozen years younger, was risk-averse. AJ could draw, but his takeout weight was timid, and the results were less than useful.

Jamie was streaky when it came to draw weight, but he was a master take-out artist. As a pair team, AJ and Jamie did quite well by doing the Canadian thing and meeting halfway. This season, they were aiming for the top – the Southwestern Saskatchewan Curling Championship to be decided at a week-long bonspiel in March, called The Turkey Shoot. Randy and AJ were determined to be in contention at that tournament, maybe even take top spot. It could happen. Their motto was: Play every game as if it were the championship final.

Jamie was a jock. Even at the advanced age of 39, he was still a solid second baseman for pickup baseball and not a bad defenceman on his geezer hockey team. AJ wasn't athletic at all. He couldn't hit a baseball, even when it was placed on a waist-high tee in front of him. He couldn't catch or field, and he ran like a duck. He also couldn't skate, and he sucked at basketball. As a kid, AJ had pretty much given up on sports of any kind, when he had an epiphany in Grade Five.

His class went on a field trip to the curling rink, and AJ knew he was home. He understood the game immediately, understood the object, the strategy, and the sheer simple Scottish beauty of it. Send a granite stone roaring down a sheet of pebbled ice in such a way that it pirouettes into a twelve-foot bullseye 150 feet away, preferably knocking out an opponent's stone that is already there. To AJ, it was elemental. Rocks on ice.

AJ wanted Jamie to raise one of their rocks about two feet. Jamie wasn't particularly good at raising – using one stone to bump another further into the house and better scoring position. Almost everyone agrees, it's the toughest shot in curling, demanding pin-point accuracy, and perfect weight. Otherwise, all hell breaks loose and you wind up knocking your own stones out of contention or bumping the other guy's closer to the button. Jamie had other ideas.

"Which one's shot?" he hollered.

"This here," AJ called back, poking his broom handle at the shot rock, an opposition yellow stone in the best scoring position just inside the eight-foot ring.

"So, what if I could take it out, maybe roll in on the button?" Jamie asked. He wasn't much of a raiser, but he was a damned good take-out man.

"I don't mind that," AJ called to Jamie at the other end of the ice. "It could work. I don't hate it."

He didn't like it either. Too risky. But it was also risky to say anything like that to Jamie and maybe put him off his game. So, AJ turned his broom head vertically as a target to give Jamie just enough room to get their red stone past a yellow guard for the takeout.

At the other end of the sheet, Jamie paused, squinted down the ice at AJ's broom, squatted, and put his right foot in the left hack. He tipped his red rock, polished the bottom with his glove, and then put the rock back down on the ice, turned the handle to ten o'clock, and pushed off. As he glided down the ice, he switched the handle to two o'clock, then back to ten, and gave the rock an extra little nudge as he released it just before the near hog line. The red rock rumbled straight down the ice just to the right of the centre line. As it reached the far hog line, it started to curl but slowed down. AJ had to sweep furiously to help it slip into the eight foot, where it sent the yellow rock caroming out of play, then curled neatly into the four foot, as foretold. With the yellow rock out of play, another red rock in the twelve-foot counted as well. Final score, four to two for AJ and Jamie. AJ came slip-sliding back down the ice, and all four players shook hands.

"Good game," they murmured to each other like a secret password. "Good game."

High fives are rare in curling and are usually only seen on TV, which is to league curling what the NHL is to beer league hockey. Most curlers are deferential, not demonstrative. When they win, they are apologetic, and when they don't, they are always ready to take the blame and, like good Canadians, apologize into the bargain.

Before the four players left the ice, they pushed the red and yellow rocks back into two neat rows on either side of the hack, ready for the next game.

"Want a coffee?" AJ asked when they left the rink for the warmth of the little bistro on the other side of the glass.

"You bet," Jamie said. "Maybe that storm outside'll blow itself out if we fart around in here long enough. And maybe I'll get one of those donuts if they have any left." Amelia had been on his case about his sweet tooth, but Jamie was still as lean as he was in his twenties and used sugar as a fuel, like beef or beer.

"Hey, you guys," said Scott as AJ and Jamie came into the café.

"Hey, Pops," said AJ. "Come and join us?"

"Yeah, I got time for a coffee before our game. Molly OK?"

"Out to here and healthier than ever," AJ said, his arms cradling an imaginary pregnant belly. "She's into those fruit things she whips up in the blender, and she's just glowing." AJ wasn't big into smoothies, but he couldn't deny that his wife looked terrific.

They'd just taken their snacks to a little booth by the window when the glass splintered into lethal shards, clattered onto the tabletop, and then onto the floor, followed by torrents of wind-blown snow. The lights dimmed, flashed, and went out as the coffee shop shook like an earthquake had sundered the ground. But this was Saskatchewan, where quakes were non-existent. They scrambled out of the booth, headed for the exit, and then held the door for Jolene, Erik the cook, and two other customers. Once outside, they all looked around for the source of the upheaval.

Across the street, the wind whipped away black smoke as it billowed from a shattered window on the second floor of the Mayfair Apartments. The sky was already clearing to faded prairie blue as the roiling clouds of a fast-moving thunderstorm scudded northwest to Tuxford. The wind died to almost nothing, and a few fat flakes of snow swirled in the still air. People in the street were unsure of where safety might be. Inside? Outside? Flat on the ground? A small, dark man leading a horse and cart wove slowly in and out of the crowd, repeating a simple rhyme in a sing-song voice.

"Spare the rod and share the blame. Watch the world go up in flames. Your protection or your shame. Take the rod and fire's tamed." People in the crowd shifted to make way for the little procession. On the side of the cart was a sign:

THORSON LIGHTNING RODS

Firefighters arrived almost immediately and were already climbing the ladder as it was hydraulically raised to the second-floor window. On the ground, hydrants dribbled water until hose couplings were cinched tight. There would be a lot of ice later on. AJ was amazed that the water was flowing at all, it was so damned cold.

"Sounded like an explosion, eh," Jamie said.

"Maybe a gas leak?" AJ had been terrified of gas ever since he was a kid and failed to light the pilot light on the kitchen stove. He could smell the gas seeping into the room and was convinced the house would be blown to smithereens, so he ran outside and into the arms of his mother.

"Hey, hold on little man. Where's the fire?" Alice had laughed, catching him as he pelted down the back stairs.

"Inside!" AJ told her breathlessly. "Inside is gonna blow up. The gas." He was almost incoherent with fear.

"What gas? The stove?"

"The pilot light. It didn't."

"Light?"

"Yeah."

"It's OK, sweetie," Alice laughed. "There's a valve that shuts off the gas if that happens. And it happens a lot. Happens to me all the time."

"The house won't blow up?"

"The house won't blow up. But come on, let's go open some windows just in case."

Despite his mother's assurances, AJ had been hinky about gas ever since.

"Nah," Scott said now. "Gas lines were taken outta there a coupla years ago after another little explosion. Place seems kinda prone to them. I recall there was some litigation to that effect a while back."

"Blown 220 circuit maybe?" AJ asked, looking at the blackened stucco walls across the street.

"Yeah, maybe."

One of the firefighters came back down the ladder carrying a smoldering blanket, which he showed to the fire chief.

"No occupant at home, boss. Apartment was empty, but I think this is the culprit," he said to the chief when he got down. "One of those grounding blankets. Plugged into the AC during a thunderstorm. Recipe for disaster."

As the firefighters mopped up the scene, Scott, AJ, and Jamie went back into the curling rink café and helped Jolene clean up the broken glass and debris, then taped a big piece of cardboard over the broken window.

"What's a grounding blanket?" AJ asked.

"Don't get me started," Jamie said. "Alison and all her teenage friends are into that woo woo shit like crystals and incense and these bloody grounding blankets."

"What do they do?"

"It's like a blanket that supposedly connects you to the earth," Jamie said. "Plugs into the ground outlet of a wall socket. Supposed to help with healing or something.

Alison showed me some brochures, but it sounded like bullshit to me."

"You plug it in?"

"Yeah."

"Like an electric blanket, then?"

"Yeah, I guess so. I don't know, that's what Alison says anyway. She's always going on about it, and her mother kind of encourages her."

"Is that part of this New Age craze?"

"Yeah. Spiritual chakras or some such. Neutralizing free radicals. What do I know?"

"Boring music, from what I've heard," said Scott.

"Well, it's meant to relax you, I guess, but it just puts me to sleep."

"Maybe that's the idea."

"Thanks for helping with the cleanup, boys," Jolene said, coming out from behind the counter where she'd been mopping up some of the melted snow that had come in through the broken window.

"Hey, Jolene, you want we should put in a new pane of glass for you? Do it for nothin'." Jamie was a pretty good carpenter, and AJ could wield a hammer.

"Thanks, guys but insurance is coming over in an hour and then I'll get Randy to do it." Randy Millbank ran Painless Panes and worked around the clock if necessary. "So, you heard what the explosion was from?"

"Blown circuit?" Scott guessed.

"Thundersnow," Jolene said it like it was a fact.

"Which is…. ?"

"It's a thunderstorm during a snowstorm," Scott said. "Builds up some kind of static electricity or something. Doesn't usually hit the ground but sometimes it does. My brother Michael heard about it from the Cree. Quite powerful."

"And it hit the apartment building, attracted by the grounding blanket?" Jamie was trying to put the disparate information together. "Like the blanket was a target, a lightning rod?"

"Dee dee dee dee. Dee dee dee dee," AJ started doing the theme from *The Twilight Zone*. "Too woo woo for you, right Jamie boy?"

Chapter 28

Dear Sir or Madam, will you read my book? It took me years to write, will you take a look? It's based on a novel by a man named Lear. And I need a job so I want to be a paperback writer...

- The Beatles

The radio in Siggy's bookshop was on constantly. Sometimes, he listened to classical music on the CBC or the news programs out of Regina. Today, there was the story of the so-called Munsinger Affair in Ottawa, involving a German prostitute and spy, who was mistress to the Canadian Associate Minister of National Defense – an actual sex scandal in sleepy old Ottawa. Imagine! Meanwhile, a man who tried to blow up the Parliament Buildings died when his bomb exploded prematurely. Thousands of American draft dodgers were slipping across the Canadian border to avoid being sent to Vietnam, where a hundred American soldiers a week came home in body bags.

American cities were burning, and civil war was in the air. Meanwhile, Canada was getting ready to host the world next year at EXPO 67 in Montreal, while the separatist group Front de Libération du Québec (FLQ) was planting bombs in Westmount mailboxes.

When the never-ending litany of world problems got to be too much, Siggy turned to the pop stations to lighten the mood. It was 1966, and music was fun again. Or at least not sappy. The year started with Simon and Garfunkel's, *Sounds of Silence* – three minutes of acoustic angst – topping the Billboard charts. For the rest of the month, it alternated at Number One with the Beatles', *We Can Work It Out*. The Beatles also released their seminal album *Rubber Soul,* the Rolling Stones had a hit featuring an Appalachian dulcimer, Dmitri Shostakovich, wrote the *Cello Concerto No. 2 in G Major* and the *String Quartet #11 in F Minor*. Jazz sax giant, John Coltrane, tried LSD and released five albums.

Like music, the book business was booming. James Baldwin, Ursula K. Le Guin, Alice Munro, John Updike, Margaret Atwood, Joseph Heller – so many writers were at the top of their game and book sales had never been higher. Siggy had to expand the shelving in the store at the expense of one of the easy chairs and spent most of his days on the phone ordering books or phoning people to tell them that their books had come in. Some books never even made it onto the shelves; they were sold right out of the packing box. Not a bad problem to have.

The bookstore shared the block with a dry cleaner, a drug store, a shoe store, and a laundromat. Main Street hadn't changed much since Siggy first opened the bookstore more than twenty-five years ago. He marvelled at that number. A quarter of a century. Almost half his life. He never expected to be in business for so long. He never expected to be in business at all, just like he never expected to go to war or have a wife like Alice or a son like AJ. A guy would give his left leg for a life like that. Wouldn't he?

"You sleepin'?" Ab Hildebrandt asked, peering at Siggy over the counter.

"Huh? Oh, sorry, Ab. I was miles away. How're ya keeping?"

"Oh, you know. Keepin' outta trouble. Mostly ennaway, heh heh." Since Ab retired from the CPR half a dozen years ago, he'd been slowly moving his collection of books into the library in Crescent Park. The librarian asked him to give a couple of talks about the collection, and Ab was suddenly the darling of the Moose Jaw literary set. He also attracted the attention of a few women of a certain age who ensured that he was well fed and cared for.

"Got a book you might like, Ab," Siggy said, pulling a copy of Poul Anderson's *The Corridors of Time* from underneath the counter. "This'll really mess with your head. It's about these pathways that connect different ages, different eras, so people can go back and forth in time." Siggy was always finding new books for Ab to read, after Ab had so generously shared his library for all those years.

"I thought I'd read pretty near every book worth reading, but you keep coming up with new ones," Ab said. He enjoyed talking with Siggy about what they'd been reading. As Ab was slowly divesting himself of books, Siggy was acquiring more all the time.

"Well, they just keep writing them, so what else can I do?" he said. "It's my job!"

"What would you do if you could time travel, Siggy?" Ab was a big science fiction buff, saying it was the best American literary form of the 20th Century, far more interesting than the Beat poets or angst-ridden coming-of-age novels.

"Might go back to France in early 1941 and see if I couldn't manage to keep my left leg," Siggy said with a wry grin. "But then I'd never have had this bookstore."

"You're sure a glass half full kind of a guy, ain't ya?" Ab laughed. "Thanks for the book. I'll drop by next week, and we can talk about it, OK?"

Ab never finished the book. He fell asleep reading it and never woke up. In his memory, an easy chair was placed in a quiet corner of the library, surrounded by shelves of his books.

Chapter 29

August 6, 1975 – A tornado swept through the Canora, Burgis, and Donwell areas, destroying granaries, garages, and other buildings, up-rooting trees and damaging the branches of many others. It was accompanied by heavy rain and hail that destroyed grain crops...

AJ Siggelow wasn't going to let a little weather ruin his picnic. Canora was two hundred miles to the northeast, and the summer storm would blow itself out long before it reached Moose Jaw. He and Molly had a cooler full of fried chicken, a tub of potato salad, and half a dozen ice-cold Molsons. Henry and Rachel were teenagers now and quite happy to have the house to themselves for the day. AJ had sold his '49 Merc to a collector and, like a good, responsible family man, bought a 1971 Volvo station wagon, the 'safest car on the road' according to the salesman.

They pulled out of Moose Jaw just after nine that bright August morning and headed east along the Trans Canada then north on SK 641, a gravel grid road leading through Pense and down into the Qu'Appelle Valley.

"See, that's Joe Fafard's foundry just off of Front Street," Molly said as they drove through Pense. "He's that sculptor I was telling you about who makes the coolest critters around. Cows. Horses. Wolves. They look so real."

"Even I've heard of him," AJ said. "And he lives here?"

"Well, his foundry's here. I think they have a farm somewhere between here and the valley. I got a tour of this place during that art course I took in Regina a few years ago. Very cool how they make the sculptures. I won't bore you talking about the lost wax process, but trust me, it's very cool."

AJ didn't know anything about the lost wax process and didn't want to. He was uncomfortable in art galleries and other cultural venues, so Molly spared him the details and pursued her love of the arts on her own. AJ had lots of other fine qualities, including being a terrific father and earning a good living as a mechanic.

It was a random Wednesday afternoon in August, and they'd both taken the day off. The weather was perfect and business was slow at McKenzie Mechanical because most people were out of town, towing trailers and boats to vacation spots all over Saskatchewan to take advantage of the short, hot summer.

Molly worked when she wanted to, which was most of the time. Demand was growing for her books for children, but they couldn't be rushed. Part of their charm was that she took time and care to write the stories and paint the whimsical watercolour paintings that illustrated the books. Ironically, the fact that the books were not churned out by the millions drove up demand. But demand be damned. Molly declared August 6 'Robert Mitchum Day' in honour of the antihero movie star of the forties, fifties, and sixties, a guy who smoked pot and told reporters that all of the other rumours they'd heard about him were true, too. Robert Mitchum Day was probably a national holiday in Connecticut, where he was born, so it seemed like a good excuse to take the day off and go for a ride in the country.

It had been a good summer so far, with rain at the right times and plenty of sunshine, so the crops were in good shape. The wheat developed plump heads that were slowly turning to gold under the summer sun, a second cutting of hay was ready for harvest, and the broad fields of yellow canola flowers had set seed and were beginning to fade, although their pungent fragrance still hung in the air. As Molly and AJ drove down into the Qu'Appelle Valley, the land was still lush and green despite the hot, dry summer. They stopped for a picnic in the park in Lumsden and were just packing up to continue their journey when a small, dark man leading a horse and cart came slowly into the park. On the side of the cart was a sign:

THORSON LIGHTNING RODS

As he walked, the man repeated a verse in a droning sing-song voice: "Spare the rod and share the blame. Watch the world go up in flames. Your protection or your shame. Take the rod and fire's tamed."

Molly and AJ watched him circle once through the park, then got in the car and drove away. But somehow the day had turned. The air was cooler, damp, and clammy. Heavy black clouds rolled in quickly from the northeast and ripples of lightning flickered from cloud to cloud as the far-off grumble of thunder grew louder.

"Guess I shoulda believed the weather report," AJ said. "Is it too late to go back and buy a lightning rod from that guy?"

"Maybe we head back," Molly said. Saskatchewan thunderstorms could be violent and capricious, and it was best to stay out of their way.

"Not much point," AJ said from behind the wheel. "Storm's moving fast, and we'd be up on the flatlands when it hit. Better to be down here in the valley." He steered the

Volvo along a gravel road that led down to the river and parked beside a sheltered picnic area.

"Are you scared?" AJ asked as they hunkered down beside a cutbank.

"Not really," Molly said. "It either has your number on it or it doesn't."

"That's pretty brave talk. Your uncle got killed by lightning, didn't he?"

"And my grandfather, and great-grandfather," Molly reminded him. "And you've had a narrow escape too."

"Do you believe what they say? About firstborns and all? I mean, we're both firstborns, and I already got hit by lightning."

"You mean the McKenzie Curse?" Molly's laugh always sounded to AJ like water rippling over stones in a brook. "Nah! That's a bunch of..."

A flash of light roared immediately above them, the sudden wind battered the trees, and fat drops of rain soaked them to the skin in seconds. They hugged each other tight, terrified by the power around them. AJ thought of pilot William Rankin falling 50,000 feet through all kinds of weather and figured if he could survive, then they could ride this one out. How long he and Molly clung to each other was hard to say – a few minutes, an hour, an eternity. The fury of the storm blurred the landscape as it washed everything clean, then huffed off to the southwest as fast as it had arrived.

"Can you hear?" Molly asked. "My ears are ringing like the bells of St Andrew's."

"You're shivering," AJ said. "Let's get the blanket from the back seat of the car."

They wrapped themselves in the musty old Hudson Bay blanket and looked around. Twigs and branches littered the ground, and large pools of rainwater reflected the steel gray sky.

"Smell the petrichor?" Molly asked.

"The what?"

"Petrichor. It's that earthy smell that comes after a rain. Like positive ions or something."

"You know the most amazing things," AJ said, kissing her. "And I want to always be with you."

"Well, so far so good, boyo," Molly said. "If we can get through a lightning storm together, we can get through anything. And now we've got something to tell the kids."

Chapter 30

Every time Amelia heard the call of a loon, she thought of Rick Moranis and Dave Thomas on Saturday Night Live. They played a couple of Canadian hosers named Bob and Doug in a skit called The Great White North, which opened with the call of the loon: *Coo loo coo coo, coo roo coo coo!* It didn't sound much like a loon, but for a while, it was the call of Canadians everywhere, a part of the shorthand language of TV tropes like Mork's *nanu nanu* signoff. This particular loon was perched on a rock on the shore of Lake Waskesiu. The water was calm and flat with a bit of mist, and the morning air was sweet and still. The peace was sublime.

Amelia had been planning this solo canoe trip for months, to get a break from what Zorba the Greek described as "... children, house, everything. The full catastrophe." She would turn fifty next year and knew she might never again get the chance to escape from her life. She loved Jamie completely and forever, and she would die or at least walk across burning coals for Alison and Zach. The two dogs, Homer and Archie, were adorable, but also a hell of a lot of work. During the day, she escaped to her job as a copywriter for ArtTalk, which fed her brain and fattened their bank account. Her Day-Timer was full of multi-coloured sticky notes adding to the already existing information about urgent appointments that demanded her attention. She never understood the colour language of sticky notes. Were green ones good and red ones bad? Stop and go? What about yellow? No doubt someone would call a meeting about it any day now.

The year 1976 was all so very much ever so, and she wanted off the merry-go-round for a while. So, she booked a cabin for a week at Lake Waskesiu, three hours north of Moose Jaw and home to elk, deer, fox, all manner of birds, and hardly any people. The chain of lakes were perfect for paddling a canoe.

After three days, her muscles were used to the repetitive movement from hours of dipping the oar in the water, her legs were tawny and taut, and her general outlook on life had improved substantially. Kev, the name she gave to her Kevlar-reinforced fibreglass Clipper canoe, was agile on the water, easy to maneuver, and light enough to carry cross-country if she had to. She'd already explored the smaller lakes closest to the cabin and was venturing further afield. All the tourist brochures advised her to visit

Grey Owl's cabin above Kingsmere Lake. Grey Owl also had a cabin in Riding Mountain National Park in Manitoba. Sounded to Amelia like a franchise, and she wanted nothing to do with it. Instead, she paddled up through The Narrows to a long stretch of Waskesiu, where she could almost reach out and touch the shore on either side. There wasn't even a loon to break the majestic silence, just the sploosh and swish of her paddle rippling the glassy water. A sandbar and a grove of trees on her left looked like a good place for lunch, so she paddled into ankle-deep water, then hopped out and hauled Kev up onto the shore.

The sun was warm, and the blue sky was just brilliant enough. Cottonwoods and pines filtered the hot August sun, and the rainbow air sparkled with refracted light. Amelia sat on a log beside Kev and opened her rucksack to find something for lunch. She ate lightly on these trips, mostly fruit, cheese, and crackers. And no wine, just fruit juice, which improved her sleep and her stamina. After lunch, she stretched out and, using her life jacket for a pillow, lay back and drowsed in the pleasant warmth of late morning. The afternoon would be hot, especially out on the lake with no shade, but she still had time for a quick snooze before paddling back to the marina.

The tap-tap-tapping of a pen became the clackety-clack of a keyboard as unreadable words floated in the misty air. Someone laughed, a shrill, bird-like rasp that contained no humour. Drops of water splattered her face as Amelia awoke to a pelting rainstorm and dark clouds, low enough to touch. She got up quickly and hauled Kev further up onto the sand, turned him over, and stashed her rucksack and life jacket underneath. The rain was driving hard now, and she was soaked through. The lake that had been calm an hour ago was roiling with white-capped chop from a wind scudding in from the southeast. A slash of lightning arced across the sky overhead, and the thunder was only three Mississippis away. Amelia wrestled a small blue tarp from underneath Kev, slung it over her head, and settled in to wait out the deluge.

Saskatchewan is a drama queen when it comes to weather. Rainfall in Saskatchewan is rare, but when it comes, it's Biblical, missing only the frogs. Wind is life-threatening, picking up grain bins and sheds, and hurling battered vehicles around the landscape like a petulant child. Summer heat is hellish, airless, dry, and full of sand. Winter cold will freeze your lungs in a matter of seconds. To stay alive in Saskatchewan was to be in constant survival mode. But she'd been through enough summer storms to know that Saskatchewan may have meteorological fits of pique, but they are short-lived, so she bided her time.

Overhead, the cottonwoods sighed and bent and creaked together under the force of the storm. Amelia was alert for any sharp cracks from breaking branches above as she watched the wind herd the waves on the lake, pushing them this way and that according to some inner wind logic. Or maybe it was just physics. The temperature had dropped ten degrees, and she shivered a little from the damp, and worried that Jamie would be worried for her if he knew about the storm.

"What if you're out there and all hell breaks loose?" he asked her as she loaded up her Subaru before setting off earlier in the week.

"You worry too much," she assured him. "I have everything I need – foul weather gear and enough trail mix to survive a month."

"Don't make light of this," he said. "People get lost all the time. Just last year..."

"Relax, my love. The big bad wilderness is not gonna get me!" And she gave him a kiss to shut him up. At sixteen, Alison was indifferent to her mother's adventures and far more interested in her pals and their constant talk about music and boys. Zach, at thirteen, wanted to come with her.

"It'd be great, Mom. Just me and you. Like a couple of explorers." She had to restrain him from running upstairs and packing his bag.

"As much as I love you," she said gently, "this is my time alone. And anyway, you'd be bored in five minutes. There's no TV up there, you know." Zach looked at her for a long minute with those hazel eyes, and then his sunny face broke into a smile.

"OK, have a good time then," he said with a quick hug before darting off down the street where a road hockey game was getting underway.

"You've got everything you need? Water? Sunscreen? Your thyroid pills?"

"Yes, mother hen.   You can stop clucking. I'll be just fine. There are stores and gas stations and electricity up there you know. There is even a TV in my cabin. I can take care of myself, much as you may think it's your job."

"I know babe, but..." Jamie turned fifty last year and had already lost some of his risk-taking spirit.   Now he just wanted everyone to be safe.

"No buts, ifs, or ands," Amelia laughed. "I'm outta here. Love y'all!" She backed out of the driveway and drove away into the summer morning.

For some reason, men always wanted to take care of her, to keep her from real or imagined harm. As a girl, it was the same story when she wanted to go riding on Blaze. After encouraging her to get the horse, her father would not allow her to go much further than the road unless someone was with her.

"What if Blaze got spooked or something?" Michael asked her.

"She'd get spooked whether someone else was there or not," Amelia reasoned. "So, it's down to how good a horsewoman I am." In the end, she went riding on her own, fell a few times, and kept all her injuries a secret from her parents except for a hard-to-hide broken wrist. Now, she peeked out from under her tarp to discover that the rain had let up and the steady dripping was from the cottonwoods overhead. She stood up, shook the water off like a spaniel, and tipped Kev onto his keel. After loading him up, she pushed off into the water and started paddling southeast toward the marina where she'd parked the car.

Coo loo coo coo, coo roo coo coo! The loon that welcomed her earlier that morning was still on his rocky perch as she paddled back down the lake. Far away, the storm grumbled as it lumbered off to the northwest, an occasional flash of lightning flickering between the bruised thunderheads. She could see the marina now, the parking lot deserted except for her red and black Subaru wagon. All the other boaters must have fled back into town for burgers and beer before the storm hit.

As she paddled for home, a knife of sound slashed across the sky, the brilliant air crackled around her, and the world held its breath for a moment too long.

~ The End ~

En-lightning Facts and Fancies

Since the dawn of time, humans have been in awe of lightning's power, and over the centuries, we have personalized the gods who hurl thunderbolts at us. The Greeks fear Zeus and Pegasus, the winged horse that carries his lightning bolts. The Scandinavians invoke Thor, and Slavic people look to Perkūnas to fight on their behalf against the devil. Native Americans revere Thunderbird, lightning-breathing dragons control the Chinese weather, and the African Bantu fear the anger of lightning god Kiwanuka. These gods toss around bolts that turn buildings into kindling and set forests on fire. Even Santa Claus harnesses lightning with his reindeer, Donner (Thunder) and Blitzen (Lightning).

We have woven lightning into our mythology as an omen, as retribution for some imagined sin, or even as a holy signal from the great beyond. We regard lightning as a supernatural, otherworldly event, the gods reaching through the scrim of the world to show us their powers.

The National Oceanic and Atmospheric Association – the weather people in the

United States – groups lightning into five main types:

Cloud to Cloud Bolts, sheets, or shimmers of electricity that stay within the cloud mass or between clouds

Cloud to Ground A charge from a storm cloud that spikes down to the ground in a zig-zag pattern, sometimes striking taller objects such as trees or telephone poles.

Heat Lightning Flashes (sometimes reddish) that are too far away for the thunder to be heard

Sprites Flashes of just a few seconds above a storm cloud, often at the same time as cloud to ground lightning

Elves Glowing areas hundreds of miles across that last a thousandth of a second above areas of cloud to ground lightning

Myths and Facts

Fact: Canada averages more than two million cloud-to-ground lightning strikes every year, according to Environment Canada. The busiest month for lightning is July. Most lightning strikes occur between one and six p.m.

Fact: Saskatchewan is one of the most lightning-prone places on earth, with more than 600,000 strikes every year, most of them in the summer.

Fact: Four times as many men as women are hit by lightning, according to the US Center For Disease Control, which also reports that the average age of a person struck by lightning is 37. There is a one in a million chance of a person being struck by lightning in any given year. Ninety per cent of the victims survive.

Myth: Lightning never strikes the same place twice.

Fact: The lightning rod on top of the Empire State Building in New York City is hit as often as a hundred times a year, and in 2010, it was struck three times in one night. In 2023, Li Shifu of Zunyi, Guizhou, was struck twice in the space of five minutes. And Roy Cleveland Sullivan, a park ranger in Shenandoah National Park in Virginia, claimed to have survived seven lightning strikes over the course of his life. He died at the age of 71 of a self-inflicted gunshot wound.

Myth: To quote Fleetwood Mac: "Thunder only happens when it's raining."

Fact: Lightning can come from a clear sky, literally a bolt from the blue. 'Positive lightning' may originate in a storm miles away. It travels horizontally and then suddenly blasts into the ground.

Myth: Lying flat on the ground is the best place to be during a lightning storm.

Fact: Lying flat on the ground could expose more of your body to ground lightning. The 'lightning crouch' – basically curling up in a fetal ball – is recommended by some to decrease your contact with the earth.

Myth: Trees offer protection during a lightning storm.

Fact: Trees are among the tallest things around and are more likely to be struck by lightning, which could send large branches crashing down on your head. As the song says: "When you hear it thunder, don't run under a tree…"

Myth: Firstborns are prone to being struck by lightning.

Fact: There is no empirical evidence to suggest firstborns are more prone.

Paul Grant grew up in Vancouver, left home at fifteen and wandered around the US and Canada for a decade working as a window washer, TV extra, factory drone, landscaper, library helper, and musician. More by luck than good management, he became a journalist, writing for *The National Post* and *The Globe & Mail*. For thirty years, Paul hosted and produced shows for CBC Radio in Charlottetown, Regina, and Vancouver.

Paul is the author of *Notorious ~ A Moose Jaw Mystery* (BWL 2025) about meth, a pandemic, money laundering, real estate, and an almost forgotten Baltic war.

Paul and his wife, Laurie Dickson, wrote *The Stanley Park Companion* (Bluefield 2003), a natural and social history of Vancouver's thousand-acre back yard. Their travel blog *Road Apples* is at: https://saskwatchers2019.blogspot.com/
Paul and Laurie live in Moose Jaw.

9 780022 863538 3